SCHOOLBOY CRICKET HEROES

By

John Costello

JAYCEE BOOKS

ISBN 0–9525773–2–1

Cover illustration by Charlie Turner

Published by Jaycee Books
Typeset, printed and bound by J. W. Arrowsmith Ltd, Bristol

Contents

CHAPTER ONE

Beginnings

Young Mark Adams could not understand why there was no organised cricket played at his junior school. He also wondered why there was an absence of this particular sport at other junior schools in the area of Wufton, his hometown.

"It's not *fair*, Dad," Mark complained to his father concerning this matter one day a fortnight before the start of the cricket season. "*You* played cricket at school at my age, didn't you?"

They were eating breakfast in the kitchen of their small terraced house. Outside, the morning sun shone brightly through the bay window that looked out onto the lawn and small back garden, at the bottom of which ran a railway line leading to North of the country in one direction, and to London, the other. A train sped by now, disturbing the silence of the early morning and interrupting also the conversation between Mark and his father for a brief moment.

"Yes, Son, I most certainly did play the game at school at your age," his father finally answered, looking deep into Mark's questioning bright blue eyes. Then, by way of a sympathetic explanation, added: "Believe me, I am concerned that you're being denied this privilege I was fortunate enough to have had; but I'm afraid it's just the way things are these days, Mark."

Young Mark still did not understand. "How do you mean?" he questioned his father's unsatisfactory answer further.

After all, other sports at his school were still played. Football.

Swimming. Athletics. All of which he participated in. So why not cricket? His father finished drinking his coffee. He would be leaving for work shortly, therefore denying Mark this opportunity of an in depth discussion on the subject.

From the top of the stairs his mother's voice suddenly called to him: "Have you finished eating your breakfast, Mark? Hurry up! You'll be late for school."

He gulped his glass of milk down. Mark had no intention of being late. He liked school very much; but this business of cricket, or the lack of it where he was concerned, he took very seriously indeed and would have liked the opportunity to discuss it further with his father. Another time perhaps when they were both not quite so rushed?

"Times have changed since my days at school, Son," Mark's father offered a final explanation to his dilemma, slipping on his jacket. "There aren't the sport's masters interested enough to devote the time and energy needed to run a school cricket team like there was when your Uncle Frank and I were your age, Mark. They also expect to be paid for any out of school activities these days. No – as I say – I do sympathize with you, but I'm afraid it's a sign of the times."

Mr. Adams picked up his briefcase from behind the sofa, shouted: "Goodbye, dear!" to his wife upstairs, and left the house uttering the following words of advice to his son: "I shouldn't worry yourself too much about this business, Mark. After all, it is your schooling that should be your main concern. You will be eleven years old this coming Saturday and you need to concentrate on your forthcoming exams. This should be your main priority. Anyway, there are other sports at your school besides cricket that you could become involved with, isn't there?"

With that, his father departed, leaving Mark none the wiser and feeling thoroughly dejected concerning his innocent enquiry about there being no cricket at his junior school. Mark wondered whether it was the same in other parts of the country? If so, was it any wonder there were no longer the youngsters showing an interest in the game like they once did? It didn't make sense. After all, where were the young England players of the future coming from if the game itself was not being encouraged at this level? Couldn't anyone see this?

Well, Mark could see it all right, so much so, that he became very disillusioned with all grown ups – especially parents and teachers – as they seemed only interested in going to work and watching television in his opinion. Any activity other than this was taboo to them. Which was a shame, because he felt he was undoubtedly missing out, as were indeed all boys of his age group where playing the game of cricket was concerned. No one – least of all parents or teachers – it seemed, was remotely interested in their predicament.

Perhaps he should confide in his mother with the problem? He knew though that it was out of her jurisdiction really, the game of cricket not being one of life's priorities for her.

"Be careful crossing the road now," she warned him caringly, waving farewell to him at the door as he set off on his journey to school.

It took only ten minutes to walk the short distance from his home to Neswell Junior School, and then, as was the custom at this time of the morning, Mark would meet up with his best pal and school chum, Wesley Jackson, a West Indian boy of the same age as he. Together they would stride out along the picturesque, tree-lined pathway on their journey to school. Both were strong, healthy looking boys with dark, curly hair, sparkling eyes and mischievous smiles counselling their young, innocent faces.

Their immediate conversation upon meeting would be of their individual exploits of the weekend which would also include any particular TV or video programmes of interest they might have seen. Both were very sports orientated, and talk of how their favourite football teams faired or snooker idols progressed would normally last long enough to take them in through the school gates to their place of learning. Sometimes a cry of: "Goal! England have scored!" could be heard coming from the mouths

3

of these excitable youngsters as they kicked a stone or empty cigarette packet through the entrance of the school.

This particular morning, however, both Mark and Wesley were of a much quieter nature than usual. Both had the serious subject of cricket on their young minds. And both were most concerned that with a new season about to start, still nothing was being done to introduce the game there by anyone in this, the boy's final term at Neswell. To actually go the duration of one's entire junior schooling without ever putting bat to ball, so to speak, seemed, in their humble opinion, almost impossible to believe, considering their very sporting backgrounds. Both their father's played for local cricket clubs. And another rather astonishing fact was the knowledge that Mark's uncle Frank had once been engaged on the playing staff of the Middlesex County Cricket Club in his youth. It seemed strange that now all these years later his young nephew wasn't even yet participating in the game.

"What did your Father say then, Mark?" Wesley asked his friend after they met.

"Not much – only that it was a sign of the times about they're being no cricket at Neswell," Mark informed him sadly, "and that there were no longer the staff with time for cricket."

"Yeah – exactly what my Dad said. He says perhaps I can join the colts team next year at his club though."

The young West Indian managed half a smile that immediately lit up his dark, round face with irresistible schoolboy charm at the thought of this prospect. He went through the motions of bowling a fast Yorker with a small stone that he suddenly produced from his pocket, a perfect delivery, hitting middle stump on the trunk of an elm tree the length of a cricket pitch in front of him.

"Howzat!" he exclaimed excitedly, throwing his arms in the air, almost knocking a fellow pupil off his bike as the youngster swerved to avoid the West Indian fast bowler in jubilation at dismissing England's opening bat for a duck!

"My Dad'll probably ask me along to his club next season the same as you," Mark informed his friend of this likelihood as they strolled along the tree-lined driveway of the school entrance which was crowded now with other boys and girls at this time of day on their way to be educated.

On their left, an expanse of green field displayed a generous area for Neswell's sporting activities.

What a pity, young Mark thought to himself, that there was no area reserved for cricket here. It certainly was a very sad state of affairs, for in his mind he could picture white-clad youngsters participating in this most English of games and it made him feel very angry indeed that the education authorities in their town of Wufton could have actually allowed the beloved game to completely disappear in this way from its schools. No one, it seemed, was the least bit concerned with this present arrangement. No one, apart from himself, that is, for this particular morning it suddenly dawned on Mark as he gazed out over the school playing field that he was going to make a stand and put up a fight to protest against this absence of cricket and try and bring back the sport so that he and future pupils would benefit if he proved to be successful in achieving this aim.

"*You'll* help me, won't you, Wes?" Mark enquired earnestly of his friend, leading the way onto the grass alongside the school's football pitch. A copper-beech privet hedge separated another area of the playing field, where, according to Mark's father, the cricket square used to be situated in the past.

"With what?" young Wesley asked innocently, obediently following his friend.

Mark stood gazing out over the hedge in front of him. Yes, he could picture it now – a game of cricket in progress; the sun shining; the sound of bat on ball; of spectators applauding. Was it only a dream, or could he, a mere eleven year old, help to achieve this?

"To form a school cricket team this season, that's what!" he informed his opening bowler enthusiastically. "You interested?"

"Sure thing! Yeah, great, man! But how on earth we gonna do that?"

5

"By meeting me outside the bike shed at lunch time for a start, that's how."

The assembly bell sounded over in the school hall. The two boys scampered off down the driveway, their excited young minds full of plans with the idea of forming a school cricket team together.

CHAPTER TWO

School Policy

It was the general opinion of all teaching staff at Neswell Junior School that young Mark Adams was a bright, intelligent pupil, with an alert, enquiring mind and possessing qualities of leadership. However, even at this early age, no one at the school could have imagined how events would develop over the next few weeks concerning his involvement with the game of cricket. It proved to be an eye opener for everybody. The impact this boy was to have on everyone would be unimaginable.

After assembly that morning, Mark requested a meeting with the school's headmaster, Mr Turnbull. Permission was granted, an appointment being made immediately after lunch for him. On hearing this news, his friend, Wesley, sitting next to him in their classroom, began to feel excited with the knowledge that his friend was indeed serious with his cricket intentions.

"And what might you two be up to?" their form master, Mr Fox, enquired of them suspiciously from his position in front of the blackboard.

The eyes of fellow pupils diverted attention from their present studies to the culprits in question. Everyone was well aware that something was afoot when permission to see the head teacher was asked for by Mark earlier.

"Nothing, sir!" Mark answered for both of them with confidence.

Old Foxy (the school's nick-name for their form teacher)

looked at the pair of them warily. Past experience had taught him to beware of mischievous schoolboys. "Well, with *your* permission we *would* like to resume where we left off yesterday with the reading of Mr Charles Dickens!" he indicated to them sternly with the intention of installing a sense of discipline that otherwise had been lost by the attention Mark's request to see the head of school had made on the rest of the class. "Now – if you will all please turn to page 35 in your books . . . !"

Later that day, Mark sat in the corridor outside the headmaster's office. During the course of that morning he had taken the opportunity during some quiet moments of the Charles Dickens readings to give thought to some words of his own that he might use when putting forward his idea of forming a school cricket team to the head. He didn't feel in the least bit daunted at the prospect of confronting the man over this issue, and was quite eager to express his views on the subject to him.

"And what might we do for you, young Adams?" Mr Turnbull enquired, ushering him in to his office and to a chair in front of his desk. A window behind this desk looked out on to the school's playing field.

A tall man with thick-rimmed spectacles, the headmaster peered menacingly through them at young Mark from his authoritative position opposite; but Mark felt in no way put off or inferior by his presence.

"I was wondering, sir!" he began slowly and calmly, about to put forward his idea. "If there was any chance of forming a school cricket team this year?"

The head remained silent for a moment, his eyes fixed on those of the youngster in front of him. He began twiddling his thumbs, a smile spreading across his otherwise serious face. "A *cricket* team?" he reiterated, somewhat relived at the nature of this request. He had been half expecting something of a far more serious content, as is the usual custom with boys of his age, such as requests for transfers from one class to another for whatever reason; or by far the most popular, hand written notes from anguished parents excusing their delicate offspring from participating in physical training periods because of possible asthmatic attacks brought on by any form of vigorous exercise. But *cricket* ... ! Turnbull felt somewhat at a loss for words momentarily, this particular game not really being his forte, so to speak.

"Yes, and could you also please tell me, sir, why *no* cricket is played at other junior schools in the county any longer?" Mark questioned further in a confident manner.

The head leant back in his chair, somewhat surprised by this extensive questioning on the subject of cricket being aimed at him by this persistent youngster. Then, clearing his throat, Turnbull, to the best of his ability, offered an explanation: "In answer to your first enquiry concerning the forming of a school cricket team here at Neswell this year, Adams, well, I have to tell you quite categorically that this is hardly likely. The reason for this is because we have no form master able to take on the responsibility it would involve. Your second question as to why there is no longer any cricket played at junior school level in this area is because of a decision made by the education authorities some time back not to include the game in general sporting activities as in the past. An acute shortage of sports masters with knowledge of cricket, and a lack of interest in the game, I believe, are the reasons given for this. The lack of playing facilities needed for the game was also mentioned."

With the deliverance of these explanations given by Turnbull, a silence between master and pupil prevailed. The head teacher of his school had now repeated what young Mark had been told by his father earlier. So, could *nothing* be done to bring the game of cricket back to Neswell?

"But our school *does* have a playing field," Mark emphasised this fact hopefully, breaking an uncomfortable silence, "and cricket *could* be played here?"

"*Could* and *will* are two entirely different matters, young man; and I can assure you that there *won't* be any cricket played here at Neswell – at least – not in the foreseeable future, at any rate."

With this final statement from Turnbull, the meeting between master and pupil, it would seem, had come to its conclusion. Sad, because so far as young Mark was concerned it still left him no nearer to forming a school team. In reality, it had achieved absolutely nothing.

The head rose from behind his desk. "Believe me, I *do* understand how you must feel," he sympathised with the boy, moving in the direction of the door, indicating that their meeting was indeed at an end. "But take it from me 'there are *far* more important things in life, my lad. I suggest you channel your energies into learning. It will certainly pay dividends in the long run. After all, you have the rest of your life to play cricket, haven't you?"

Mark left the headmaster's office feeling very disappointed and thoroughly dejected. He would not, however, admit defeat and was determined, despite old grumpy Turnbull's attitude toward his cricket dream, take this issue still further.

For the moment, it meant just as far as the bike shed to meet his friend, Wesley, as arranged. The playground was crowded with other pupils enjoying the remainder of their lunch break, with groups standing around chatting, while others kicked footballs, imagining, no doubt, they were their soccer idols as seen on television screens the night before.

Wesley, though, was not among these, standing as he was propping up the bike shed waiting for his friend. His thoughts were of the school cricket team that he and Mark hoped to establish. However, he had no way of knowing the negative response that their plan had just met with. He was soon to find out though.

"Ol' Turnbull didn't wanna know," Mark informed his pal disappointedly.

"What did he say?"

"The same as *our* parents. No sports masters interested. No facilities."

"We got facilities," Wesley exclaimed enthusiastically.

"Yes," Mark agreed, "but we can't use them. Leastways, not for cricket anyway. What a waste!"

"So – what we gonna do?"

10

The school bell sounded for class assembly. Our two cricketing enthusiasts did indeed look a sorrowful pair as they slouched across the playground toward their place of learning. They were, without doubt, two very dissatisfied, unhappy youngsters regarding the head's response to their proposal.

"I'll have a word with my Uncle Frank," Mark told his friend, hopeful that he might be able to help them with their problem. Mark sincerely hoped so; for he was determined that Neswell should have a school cricket team.

CHAPTER THREE

Discussions

Mark's uncle came to see them that same evening, Friday, to discuss the possibility of taking his nephew along to Lord's cricket Ground as a birthday treat the following day to watch Middlesex play Yorkshire in a county game there.

"*Can* I, Dad?" Mark pleaded for his father's permission at the thought of this exciting prospect. "I *can* go, can't I?"

His father, seated at the dining room table and busy wading through reams of paperwork brought home from his company's insurance office, looked across at his elder brother opposite. Very similar in appearance (they were often mistaken for twins, despite the three years age difference between them) they had remained close over the years. Unlike his brother, Frank chose a bachelor's life, devoting all his spare time away from his job as an electrical manager, to that of sporting activities.

Like his brother, he also played cricket for Wufton C.C. being a very good all rounder over the years for the Club. Other active games he was involved in were golf, squash, tennis and swimming. He was also a member of the Middlesex County Cricket Club, where he had previously spent three glorious years of his youth engaged on their ground staff, and where, obviously, his cricketing roots lay. He liked to pop along to Lord's whenever possible during the season to sit in the pavilion and support his old County.

Frank and his nephew got on very well together, and, being

the youngster's birthday, he thought it was about time that Mark paid a visit to the Mecca of cricket to watch some professional cricket.

"If you promise your Uncle Frank you'll behave, I think it'll be all right, Son," Mark's father agreed to this eventful happening.

"Lords! Wow . . . !"

"I had better prepare some packed lunches for you both," Mark's mother offered, anxious that the two of them should not starve. Knowing her son's appetite the way she did, she feared this might be a possibility unless a large size hamper was on hand for him during the course of the day. She was grateful though of Frank's offer to take Mark along to Lord's with him. After all, the boy's own father wouldn't take time off from his precious work these days to do even this.

"Why don't you come with us, Jim?" Frank put to his brother seriously. "It'll be a great day out . . .."

"I wish I could," he answered, burying himself in his work. "I've got *so* much to get through here. Another time, perhaps?"

From the expression on young Mark's face, Frank could detect the lad's obvious disappointment at his father's decision. He quickly changed the subject by asking his nephew how school was these days.

"Yeah – school's all right, I suppose," Mark sighed as he remembered with sadness his meeting with Turnbull earlier that day on the matter of cricket.

"You don't sound all that happy, Mark?"

"It – it's just that no cricket's played there anymore, Uncle Frank."

"I know – a sad state of affairs, if you ask me. Unheard of in our day, eh, Jim?"

"Unbelievable, really," Mark's father agreed with his brother. "But as I said to the lad earlier, it's the way things are now. Anyway, time enough next year for cricket. In the meantime he should concentrate on his studies."

13

"But we want to form a cricket team at Neswell," Mark vigorously informed the grown ups of his intensions.

"Really . . . ?" Frank enquired questioningly.

"And *who* may I ask, is *we*?" his father asked rather sternly, looking up from his work, somewhat surprised by this remark.

"Wes and myself – we want to bring the game of cricket back to our school," Mark replied with an air of confidence.

"That's the young West Indian lad from down the road, isn't it?" Frank asked with interest. "His Father works at our place. Good cricketer, I'm told."

"He certainly is. Club's opening fast bowler. Probably come up against him this season some time, Frank? New fixture."

The thought of Wesley's father bowling to him did not capture Frank's imagination half as much as the statement from his young nephew concerning plans to introduce cricket once more at his old school. He certainly did admire his enthusiasm.

"You're really serious about this aren't you, Mark?" he questioned the boy further.

Mark moved closer to his uncle, about to put a plan he had in mind into operation now that he had gained his attention. "Very serious," he said confidently. "Uncle Frank . . . ?"

"Yes, Mark."

"Do . . . do you think *you* could help us?"

"Depends – what had you in mind?"

Mark hesitated for a moment, not sure of what his uncle's reaction might be by involving him in their scheme. He realised though that he, more than anyone, would know the right approach to adopt in questioning the authorities concerning the absence of cricket in their schools, so bravely asked him: "Could *you* have a word with our Headmaster about the forming of a school cricket team?"

Mrs Adams decided it was time for a cup of tea, so left the room, allowing the men-folk to continue talking more on their beloved subject. Not that she wasn't interested in cricket. Far from it; she loved the game, and, over the years, had supported her husband's team with avid enthusiasm. She even took on the task of preparing afternoon teas for the cricketers for three whole seasons when Jim was playing regularly for his Club. She enjoyed doing this so much that she seriously thought of getting involved again. That is, until Jim decided to accept promotion at work last year, thereby shouldering more responsibility for himself that consequently led to longer working hours and less time for him to play cricket. He participated in only three or four games last season, she remembered with a certain sadness. Not like the old days when he played regularly every weekend. They were happy, carefree days. Would they ever return? she wondered solemnly. They should, for Mark's sake. After all, he wanted cricket played at his school again and needed his father's support and encouragement. Unfortunately he wasn't getting any and had to rely more and more on his uncle for it. As a mother, she knew this couldn't be healthy for the boy. He was at the age when a strong and happy relationship with his father was of the utmost importance. She wished Jim could be more like his brother at times such as these. He seemed far more understanding and knowledgeable of the boy's feelings and desires. It was Mark's birthday tomorrow, and his own father couldn't even find the time to be with him. He had put his work before even that. She felt she wouldn't forgive her husband's uncaring and thoughtless attitude over this in a hurry. Their already strained relationship together brought on by Jim's obsession with work this past year, didn't look like improving. The atmosphere this had created in their household would undoubtedly affect young Mark. She was very concerned that Jim couldn't, or *wouldn't* accept there was a problem between them. It needed solving before getting completely out of hand.

Mrs Adams returned to the room carrying a tray with cups of tea and a plate of Mark's favourite chocolate biscuits. "I think that our Son is genuinely concerned about the future of cricket at junior school level, Jim," she contributed to the conversation in full support of Mark's beliefs, "and not just thinking of his own keen desire to play. Isn't that so, Mark?"

"Yes, that's right, Mum," Mark answered positively, helping

himself to a biscuit. "Of course, we – Wes and I – want to play cricket as soon as we can; but the way things are it's not likely there'll be any at our level again. Do you think that's right, Uncle Frank? I mean, *you* were a professional cricketer once yourself. I'm sure if you have a word with ol' Turnbull for us, he might just see things differently."

"Your Uncle has better things to do with his time than run around after you, young man," Mark's father said to him rather curtly, rummaging through his documents on the table.

Mark, however, paid no heed to his words, anxious to obtain this favour from his uncle. "Please, Uncle Frank – say you'll help us."

Frank remained silent for a while. Then, catching his brother's eye, commented: "The lad's certainly persistent, Jim – I'll say that much for him."

Jim leant back in his chair and heaved a sigh. "Yes; but as I said to him this morning – next year he'll be at senior school. Plenty of opportunity then for cricket. He'll also be eligible to play in our Colts side at the Cricket Club. I'll have more time to spend with him as well when my promotion's settled down a bit. We can both keep an eye on him then if he'll just be patient."

Frank sipped his tea. "I must admit this sort of thing wouldn't have happened when I was your age, Mark. Times certainly have changed. It does seem unfair to deprive you of your cricket in this way. But to be honest, I don't see them changing their present policy no matter what I or anyone else might say."

"No good whatsoever," Jim agreed with his brother's statement.

"But . . . .." Frank deliberated thoughtfully. "I'm willing to have a talk with your Headmaster if it will make you happy, Mark."

"Oh, great! Thanks, Uncle Frank," Mark cried joyfully, knowing that with his support on this issue it was indeed a step in the right direction.

Mark's father made no comment on his brother's decision to help his son; but deep down felt that he himself should possibly be giving the lad more support. He would have to make it up to Mark at some later date.

Mrs Adams, on the other hand, was thrilled by Frank's generosity and kindness. Perhaps now her husband might think differently with regards to where his immediate priorities lay. She sincerely hoped so anyway. Surely he must see that Mark needed some of his precious time for help and guidance on this issue?

"Now that your Uncle has agreed to help in your adventure, don't you think it's time you went to bed, Mark?" his mother tactfully put to him.

"Yes, you will need all the sleep you can get if you are to be a good all rounder, my boy," his uncle advised him.

In fact, Mark would make no objection to going to bed now that his uncle had offered to help. He couldn't wait to inform Wesley of the news in the morning.

"Oh, just one other thing, Uncle Frank," he said, suddenly remembering his good pal.

"Yes, Mark . . . ?"

"Is there any chance that Wesley can come with us to Lord's tomorrow?"

"Oh, you two boys – don't you go *anywhere* without one another?" his mother commented in good humour.

Frank finished drinking his tea. "Yes, I should think so," he replied, smiling.

"Thanks, Uncle Frank. Thanks a lot."

After bidding everyone good night, young Mark took himself off to bed, feeling extremely happy with the way the day's events had gone. He looked forward very much to the following day and Lord's!

CHAPTER FOUR

A Sleepless Night

It poured with rain all that night and well into the early hours of the following morning. There was also thunder and lightning, so much so that it prevented Mark from getting hardly any sleep. He lay in bed listening to the rain drumming on the windowpane outside. The storm did not frighten him; but did give him cause for alarm that with so much rain falling, it might possibly prevent there being any cricket played at Lord's at all the following day.

Mark could visualize the famous Ground – up till now only seen by him in photographs in his father's cricket books, and, of course, on television – being completely submerged in water. Perhaps the game might be called off in that event? What a disappointment that would be for him, especially on his birthday. He had looked forward so much to his first visit to Lord's. Surely bad weather wouldn't mar it for him now? His friend Wesley would certainly be upset if this were the case. His mother, too, who had gone to so much trouble in preparing them food for the occasion. Packing it with such loving care inside a wicker basket, she had included cheese and tomato rolls, pate sandwiches, ham sandwiches, pork pies, chicken portions, sausage rolls and pasties. Also apples, oranges, bananas, and orange and lemonade drinks. There were biscuits and cakes as well. Enough, it would seem, to feed an army; but knowing the boys appetites the way she did, Mrs Adams envisaged not one single morsel of these contents remaining by the end of the day. Included also was one

18

of her bottles of home made wine for Frank to enjoy during the luncheon interval. It would be a pity if our three cricketing enthusiasts were not allowed to indulge themselves in these delicacies as planned if indeed bad weather was to intervene.

Another flash of lightning lit up his room momentarily, this being immediately followed by a sharp clap of thunder. The heavy rain continued to fall, pitter-pattering on the leaves of the tree outside his window. The storm left him still unafraid; but gravely concerned that there would be no cricket to watch the following day because of it.

"Please, make it stop raining!'' he prayed quietly beneath the bedclothes to his maker for this miracle to happen. ''And, God, will you *please* help me to bring the game of cricket back to my school this season.''

As Mark lay in his bedroom with the storm raging outside, he was convinced that still not enough was being done to bring pressure to bear on the education authorities concerning this cricketing dream of his. He was determined to make it come true. Tomorrow would be his eleventh birthday, which meant that at the end of this term he would be leaving Neswell to attend senior school. It left him only this coming cricket season to achieve his aim.

CHAPTER FIVE

Mark's Birthday

Mark awoke early the following morning to the sounds of birds in song and with shafts of sunlight entering his bedroom from outside. He quickly jumped out of bed and drew the half open curtains of his window wide to greet this fine day. His birthday! It had actually stopped raining outside, and, hopefully, enough to allow the possibility of play in the cricket match at Lord's later. With a blue, cloudless sky above, it appeared his wish for fine weather had been granted. He couldn't wait for his Uncle Frank to arrive.

"Happy birthday, Mark!" his mother greeted him at the breakfast table with a hug after handing him his card and present.

"Yes, happy birthday, Son!" his father conveyed his good wishes to him.

Mark opened his card hurriedly, on the front of which was a picture of an appropriate colourful cricket scene. He read the signed greetings from his parents inside; then, with excitement, opened his present. His folks had bought him a beautiful leather sports holdall.

"Oh, great!" he exclaimed joyfully. "Thanks, Mum – Dad."

"Can't have you playing in the Colts side next season without a cricket bag now, can we?" his father joked good-humouredly. "Have to see about getting you kitted out with some cricket flannels as well."

Although Mark looked forward very much to a game with the

Colts and appreciated what his father was saying with regards to this, deep down he hoped and prayed that cricket would be restored at Neswell before leaving, thereby enabling him to represent his school in this sport first.

"Anyway, have a nice day at Lord's with Uncle Frank and your friend Wesley," his father continued. "Looks like nice weather for it after all that rain last night. I'm only sorry I can't be there watching with you. Perhaps another time, eh?"

Neither Mark nor his mother offered any reply to his statement. Both knew that he was far too busy with work to spend a day at the cricket. Trying to persuade him otherwise would only mean a row developing between all of them. They didn't want that. Certainly not on young Mark's birthday. Mrs Adams sympathised deeply with her son, realizing how he must be feeling. She had actually thought of accompanying the group to Lord's herself; but decided against this finally, knowing it was his father's company that Mark wanted on such an occasion.

"Well, I must be off to the office," Mr Adams stated, collecting his briefcase and hurrying out of the house, leaving Mark and his mother sitting at the table in thoughtful silence.

"Anyway...." Mark's mother finally broke this silence, reaching out to touch her son's arm affectionately. "You have a nice day at the cricket, dear. And remember to be a good lad for your Uncle now, won't you? And keep an eye on your friend Wesley. Don't want anyone getting lost, do we?"

"No, Mum," Mark answered, appreciating her concern over his day out, knowing how she must have felt about his father's attitude toward the day in general. He really did feel let down by him. Not just over Lord's either; but also by his general lack of enthusiasm to even consider meeting Neswell's headmaster to discuss the possibility of future cricket there. This task, he was quite willing for his brother to attend to, which left Mark feeling rather infuriated. If only his father would show some interest in Mark's sporting activities?

Wesley arrived bubbling with excitement at the thought of going to Lord's for the day. He wished his school chum a happy birthday, giving him a card and a cricket book for a present. Mark thanked him kindly. It was good having a friend like Wes.

Then his Uncle Frank drew up outside the house in his shiny car to take them to London. "Happy birthday, young Mark!" he congratulated his nephew with a broad smile, presenting Mark with another card to add to his collection.

"Have a nice day!" Mrs Adams waved them all farewell after they had loaded the food basket inside the boot.

The boys sat in the back of the car contemplating what sort of day lay before them as they sped along the motorway towards St John's Wood, the sun above shining gloriously.

"Hope Middlesex bat first!" Mark said excitedly, flipping through the pages of his newly acquired cricket book.

"Yeah, be great to see them in action," Wesley remarked with similar enthusiasm.

"Should be a good day's cricket if the weather holds," Frank commented, glancing at the jubilant youngsters in his driving mirror. He could well remember his very first visit to Lord's. He had been just as excited all those years ago as they were now.

"Do you really think they'll start on time after so much rain, Mr Adams?" Wesley asked politely.

"Yes, will they, Uncle Frank?" Mark enquired tentatively, fearing that the wicket might well be waterlogged.

"Yes, I think so, lads. These days the wickets are covered overnight. Not like when I was your age. Not much protection then from the weather, I'm afraid. The outfield could be a bit damp; but I'm sure there'll be no delay."

They came off the motorway and journeyed down through Swiss Cottage to arrive at Lord's fifteen minutes later. Mark was looking forward very much to watching his first professional county cricket match there.

CHAPTER SIX

Lord's

Frank parked the car and the three of them strolled round the Nursery End of the Ground, where, they observed, players from both teams were taking net practise prior to the start of the game. Both youngsters stood enthralled as they watched with other spectators gathered behind the nets at these professionals at work. To be so close to their cricketing idols was indeed a rare treat for the pair of them.

"That's Nick Gallon, the Middlesex captain in the far net," Frank informed them, and, by the sound of his voice, seemed just as excited as they in witnessing this fact.

"I know," Mark acknowledged this remark.

"And *that's* John Williams bowling to him," Wesley recognised the County's off spinner excitedly. And running in menacingly behind him came Andy Simmons, the opening Middlesex fast bowler with a delivery that beat Gallon's bat through sheer pace as it fizzed into the back netting directly in front of them.

"Wow!" exclaimed Wesley unbelievingly, a vision appearing in his mind that maybe one day he himself would be as fast as that.

"Yes," Frank sighed. "I shouldn't fancy having to face him, that's for sure."

After watching the cricketers practising for a while the youngsters then accompanied Frank on a stroll round the Ground, stopping first at the opening by the sight screens at the Nursery End to take in the pleasant view. The noble and picturesque pavilion building loomed large in front of them beyond the lush-green turf of the famous Mecca of cricket. Both Mark and Wesley stood in awe as they gazed for the first time upon the scene, taking in also the sweep of the Tavern Stand to their left, above which, gently swaying in the breeze, old Father Time stood high on his faithful perch gazing down on the scene below. Adjacent to this was the Mound Stand with its tent-like awnings high above. Following this round, their eyes then focused on the Edrich Stand to their right the other side of the opening, curving left to meet up with the Compton Stand and the tiered Grand Stand. Continuing along from here, the Warner Stand, situated to the immediate right of the pavilion, a full circumference of the sunlit ground having been viewed by the two lads. They were feeling what countless others had felt on their very first visit to Lord's.

"There's no other Ground to compare with it," Frank assured them, appreciating their emotional feelings. Hadn't he experienced the very same with his first Lord's encounter?

"Morning, Frank!" a tall, sun-tanned young man greeted Mark's uncle as he passed them by on his way out toward the wicket with six brand new cricket stumps cradled in his arms.

"Hello, Mick! How are they treating you?" Frank greeted this character warmly.

"Mustn't grumble. Nice day for it, especially after last night's deluge, eh?"

"I'll say. The boys here were worried they wouldn't see any cricket today."

The blue-eyed man, who, the youngsters guessed to be the groundsman, flashed a smile at the pair of them. "Take more than that these days to cause a delay," he assured them kindly.

Frank then introduced them, informing him that it was their first visit to the famous Ground to watch cricket.

Before departing to erect the stumps for the start of play, the man bade them farewell, saying: "I hope you enjoy a good day's cricket, boys. Middlesex won the toss and are batting, by the way."

They both thanked him, hardly able to believe that they had actually been talking to the Head Groundsman of Lord's. They felt very honoured.

"Right, then, young Mark," Frank addressed his nephew in a tone of voice that made the youngster think that perhaps another surprise was in store for them. As indeed there was; but this time it was for him alone. "Before we watch the cricket I want you to come along to the Lord's Shop to buy you a birthday present that I think you'll find useful."

"A *present*!" Mark exclaimed excitedly.

"*Great*, man!" Wesley sighed, unable to conceal his feeling of joy for his friend on this special occasion.

"We'll just have time to get it before the players come out."

The youngsters followed behind Frank obediently as they made their way toward the Lord's Shop that was situated off to the right behind the Edrich Stand.

"This was once the Head Groundsman's cottage when I was a young lad on the Staff here," Frank informed them as they stepped inside the building. "As you can see – it has now been converted into a shop. You go browse round while I sort out your present, Mark."

They did just that, fascinated with the many different cricketing items on sale. There were latest editions of various cricket books to catch the eye. Also numerous ties, sun hats, T-shirts, paintings, videos, and tracksuits. Indeed, shelves full of articles of interest to the cricket lover, all of which captivated the minds of our two youngsters with sheer delight. To them, it was tantamount with a visit to Aladdin's Cave.

"Wow!" young Wesley gasped in wonderment, his dark eyes opening wide with amazement at what they saw. "I could certainly spend some time in here."

"Yeah, me too," Mark agreed with his friend, admiring a water colour painting of the famous Lord's pavilion in front of them on a stand. "Maybe another time, eh, Wes?"

"Yeah, maybe."

Frank rejoined them, a blue nylon holdall hanging from his

clasped right hand. "Here," he said, handing it to Mark. "I hope you make good use of it."

Mark, surprised yet once again on a morning that seemed full of surprises for him, took the present from his uncle. He wanted this day to last forever and wished secretly that many more such treats were still left in store for him. "What is it?" he asked with excitement.

"I know what it is," Wesley said, just as excited as his friend and hardly able to conceal this knowledge from him. "Open it up, Mark and find out."

Mark dropped the holdall to the shop floor and unzipped it, other browsing customers in the shop looking on with amused interest as he did so. Wide-eyed, he peered inside the bag.

"There you go, man! A game of Kwik Cricket!" young Wesley confirmed this knowledge to his friend with self-assuredness.

"Look, if you turn the bag around," he continued, adjusting the holdall's position, "it says so on the front, see. . ."

Sure enough, there it was, the *Kwik Cricket* motif with its ball and stumps showing prominently on the side.

Delving inside, Mark discovered two sets of blue plastic stumps complete with stands, two sturdy blue plastic bats, two marker cones, and two red, durable lightweight balls. Also included was an instruction book explaining the rules of the game.

"I hope it gives you great enjoyment, Mark," Frank said affectionately to his nephew, looking down at him from above.

"Yeah, it's great, thanks, Uncle Frank," Mark uttered with deep sincerity, feeling quite overcome with emotion at his uncle's generosity toward him.

"I'm sure Wesley here will join in playing the game with you during your summer holiday's," Frank added, gently patting the young West Indian lad on the head.

"I sure will," Wesley admitted enthusiastically, pretending to avoid this playful gesture from the grown up; but secretly not minding it at all because he liked Mark's uncle very much and really appreciated him devoting his time in taking them to the cricket. He sure was a great sport all right. He envied Mark having such a kind and understanding uncle. Especially where cricket was concerned.

"It's great fun," Wesley added. "My Dad's Club has one of these kits. We have terrific games on the outfield after a match."

Mark fastened the bag and stood up. "But the balls are not really hard, are they?" he questioned his friend rather despondently. He didn't want to appear ungrateful with his gift. He just felt that this game was not *real* cricket somehow. Mark wanted desperately to play *real* cricket with a *real* hard ball and with a *real* bat and pads and gloves to wear. Not some sissy game like this. He began to feel guilty at having such thoughts; but couldn't help it. He just didn't feel that this was the game for him.

"Do you want to know something, Mark?" Frank addressed his nephew, sensing and understanding the comment just uttered by him. "Both your Father and I learned to play cricket with a soft ball."

"Did you, Mr Adams?" Wesley asked with interest.

"That we did – up on the estate against a lamppost. We'd spend hours there playing. And a tennis ball's all we used."

Mark was finding his confession hard to believe. "Are you serious, Uncle Frank?"

"Dead serious, lad. Yes, that's the way we learnt how to play. You see – using a soft ball teaches you to get into line for your shots when batting with no fear of getting hurt like there is with a hard ball. It also makes the bowler deliver a better line and gives the fielder confidence to catch the ball so that when you eventually do come to play with a proper leather one your techniques have been developed naturally. Believe me, it's by far the best way to learn the skills of cricket."

Perhaps Mark was trying to run before he could walk with regards to learning the basic techniques of the game? After all, if anyone should know how to go about playing cricket, surely it was his uncle. Maybe Mark should take notice of this sound advice from him.

"And do you realize . . ." Frank continued purposefully, "that this Kwik Cricket game can be played with the least amount of supervision. Which means that your dear old Headmaster would therefore probably give his permission for you to play it on your own school playing field."

Both Mark and Wesley looked at each other wide-eyed. "*Would it!*" the pair of them cried simultaneously.

"I can't see any reason why he should object."

"Then it *could* mean cricket being allowed back at Neswell after all, Uncle Frank?" Mark couldn't hide his enthusiasm at the possible prospect of this happening.

Frank placed a friendly hand on both the boys' shoulders. "Let's just say there's a distinct possibility, yes," he said, smiling. "And if you do need any help with setting it all up you can definitely count on my support."

"That's just great, man!" Wesley exclaimed excitedly.

"Yeah, thanks, Uncle Frank," Mark showed his appreciation in this matter.

"My pleasure, I can assure you. Now – let's make a move else we'll miss the cricket."

The three of them made their way round to the Warner Stand where Frank gained admission for them, purchasing a scorecard at the entrance from an M.C.C official on duty there.

Sitting in the front row with their tuck box stored safely beneath their seats, they were just in time to see the two opening Middlesex batsmen making their way down through the pavilion gates to join the Yorkshire fielding side and the two white-coated umpires already in position out on the lush-green grass. Both boys joined with Frank and other spectators in applauding the Middlesex pair.

"Here's the scorecard for the match." Frank handed this to Mark. "All the players names are there, so you will be able to follow what's going on. If you're in doubt there is the electronic Tavern scoreboard over there to put you right."

Sure enough, the names of the two Middlesex bats showed clearly on its face, as did information of who was opening the bowling for the Yorkshire side and from which end of the Ground, i.e. **P** for Pavilion and **N** for Nursery. During the course of the day they would discover other items of information as they appeared on the screen.

"There used to be a scoreboard high up to your left there before they decided to knock it down to build a new one and a new Grand Stand," Frank continued to explain the terrain of the Ground to them, memories of his youth flooding his mind in doing so. "The official scorers of the match would sit up there then to record details of everything, but I believe it's all done by computers now."

"Wow!" young Wesley uttered with amazement at the wonders of modern technology.

"Yes, I used to help operate that scoreboard when I was here on the Ground Staff," he informed the lads with a certain amount of pride.

"I bet that was interesting," Wesley said in awe.

"Terrific view, I should imagine," Mark added thoughtfully.

"Hey-up, cricket's starting."

Mark and Wesley sat glued to their seats as they watched the Yorkshire opening fast bowler run in on his way to deliver his first ball to the Middlesex opening bat facing up to him at the Pavilion End.

The pre-lunch session that they witnessed proved to be very entertaining indeed. The boys sat mesmerised as they watched in complete awe the way the professional players went about performing their craft. Mark was particularly impressed with the Middlesex batsmen as they set about executing shots, especially after a quick wicket fell, bringing his hero – Nick Gallon – to the crease. The county captain was in great form as he drove, cut, glanced, hooked, deflected, swept, punched the ball to all four corners of the Ground, the ball a red blur as it sped across the fine turf in the brilliant sunshine. He certainly kept the Tavern scoreboard blinking busily as he continued his onslaught of the bowlers, easily reaching his half-century by the luncheon interval.

Wesley, on the other hand, sat enthralled watching the fast bowlers racing in on their long, smooth run ups with their high-armed actions, amazed at the sheer pace they were able to generate. The youngster had never seen such fast bowling before in his life. It excited him greatly.

Both the lads also paid heed to the expertise of the fielding side and the manner in which they were able to stop some of the batsman's shots and return the ball to their wicket keeper with such swift accuracy. It certainly was a sight to behold, and indeed a lesson to be learnt by them if they were ever to emulate these players.

The last ball before the luncheon interval was exquisitely dispatched to the Tavern boundary by Nick Gallon for a superb four, the umpires then removing the bails from the stumps to lead the players off the field for their well earned break for refreshment.

"Are you both enjoying it so far?" Frank enquired of the youngsters who were now applauding with other spectators the players as they made their way into the pavilion.

"It's just great, man," Wesley confessed with enthusiasm, his dark eyes opened wide with wonderment at the spectacle before him.

"Nick Gallon's terrific, isn't he, Uncle Frank?" Mark's admiration for the Middlesex captain was noticeably obvious. What wouldn't he give to be able to bat like his hero?

Frank pulled the tuck-box out from under the seat. "Yes, a very forceful batsman indeed." He passed the youngsters a leg of chicken and a buttered roll to commence lunch with.

"I wish *I* was as fast as them opening bowlers." Wesley had visions of himself coming into to bowl like that in a Colt's game at his father's club.

Frank nibbled on a drumstick. "There's no reason why the pair of you shouldn't be able to play like these cricketers," he told them assuredly. "All it takes is practise and dedication. And now you have a Kwik Cricket game there should be no stopping you, should there?"

Mark and Wesley sat in silence eating their lunch and dreamed of the day when they would perform like their heroes at Lord's. But these visions of grandeur were then interrupted as a swarm of young boys and girls suddenly invaded the sacred turf at the Nursery End of the Ground armed with bats and balls. There were at least fifty of them in number as they began forming themselves into different groups, these groups then breaking away to take up positions on the four corners of the outfield where they then placed sets of the blue stumps belonging to the game of Kwik Cricket on the grass.

"Another surprise for you, lads," Frank began explaining to the youngsters as they sat gazing wide-eyed at the proceedings before them. "You are about to see a demonstration of your cricket game, Mark. It's being sponsored by the Milk Marketing Board who is introducing it to the public in this way up and down the County Grounds. There was a mention of it in the scorecard; but you obviously didn't see it."

Mark and Wesley continued eating their lunch and guzzling lemonade and looked with interest at the youngsters as they commenced to participate in this game.

"Just fancy," young Mark sighed, leaning forward in his seat and resting his hand under his chin, "all these boys and girls being allowed to play cricket at Lord's!"

"Yeah," his friend also sighed with envy, sitting next to him. "Lucky devils, aren't they?"

They watched the group in front of them by the Warner Stand enjoying a game of cricket with runs actually being scored and overs also being bowled. A scorer even sat on a small seat recording details of the match. Two umpires were also present, and keeping a watchful eye on everyone was a tall, impressive looking gentleman donned in cricket whites and wearing an M.C.C. sweater.

"Who's that, Uncle Frank?" Mark enquired. "That man in whites over there?"

Wesley also spotted him. "I bet he's a Middlesex player."

Frank knew who he was all right. He and the gentleman in question went back many years. In fact, had played for the same

M.C.C. Young Professional's side when they were on the Ground Staff together.

"He, my young friends, is Ron White – the M.C.C. cricket coach at Lord's," Frank informed them. "And if I can just catch his eye. . . I'll see if I. . ."

"Hello, Frank! How are you?" The coach recognised his old team-mate waving to him from the Stand.

"I'm fine, how are they treating you?" Frank got to his feet to shake him by the hand.

"Pretty good. What are you doing with yourself these days then?"

"Much the same, Ron. I'd like you to meet my young nephew and his friend. It's their first visit to Lord's."

Mark and Wesley were certainly meeting some interesting people today. First, the Head Groundsman, and now none other than the cricket coach at Lord's. It was all very exciting for them both.

"Pleased to meet you, lads," the man said, shaking their hands.

"It's Mark's birthday today, so I thought I'd treat him and his colleague to a day out. He's also the proud owner of a game of Kwik-Cricket, Ron."

Mark proudly pulled the holdall from beneath his seat to show it off to the gentleman.

"That's the idea, lad – you'll have some great fun with that."

"Mark and Wesley here don't have any cricket played at their school. They're trying hard to introduce it once again. Maybe they'll succeed with this Kwik-Cricket?"

"Great idea. I hope you do well with it," the coach encouraged them. Then, as an afterthought, asked: "Have you both played it before?"

"No, never," Mark confessed.

"Well, we can't have that now, can we? Fancy a kwik game then? Excuse the pun, won't you."

Both boys stood still as if frozen to the ground. Had they heard the man correctly? Did he really mean what he just said?

"Come on then you two – don't just stand there," Frank joked with them. "After all, its not every day you get asked to play cricket at Lord's, is it?"

Without further ado the pair of them stripped off their jackets and hurried through the small wooden gate that the coach held open for them on the boundary fence, then stepped out onto the sacred Lord's turf.

"Which of you does what?" the coach enquired of their cricketing abilities.

Wesley, completely overwrought with these eventful happenings and quite unable to believe that he was actually going to participate in a game of cricket at this most famous Ground, was left absolutely dumbstruck, offering no reply whatsoever to the question put to them by Ron White.

Young Mark, however, had the presence of mind to make a reply lest they were denied this unique fairy-tale opportunity offered them. "I bat – he bowls," he informed the coach hurriedly.

The coach threw Wesley a ball and handed Mark a bat to play with. Both youngsters looked at each other for a moment, unable to really believe what they were being asked to do; but then, each taking a deep breath, they threw themselves into activity with the rest of the young cricketers gathered at this corner of the Ground.

In their debut playing at the famous Mecca of cricket it didn't take the pair long to get into their stride, young Wesley bowling his fast deliveries with such excellent line and length accuracy that he was very soon rewarded with a couple of wickets, both of these being clean bowled. Mark, on the other hand, soon found his touch with the bat; executing shots all round the wicket in his total of twenty four before finally being caught out in front of the pavilion amid enthusiastic applause from the spectators witnessing these youngsters perform.

Both Mark and Wesley thoroughly enjoyed this unexpected treat for them. Well, you can imagine their exuberance at being given such an opportunity, can't you? Admittedly, their moment of glory only lasted the thirty minutes remaining before resumption of play in the County game, but never the less; the memory of it would be with them forever.

As it indeed would for Frank as he sat in the Warner stand watching with pride his young nephew participating in a friendly game of cricket with his best pal and others. Nothing like this ever happened when he was their age, that's for sure.

All too soon, however, the game came to a close when the umpire's bell on the pavilion wall tolled, summoning players and officials back for the restart of the Middlesex and Yorkshire match.

Thanking the M.C.C. coach for their game, Mark and Wesley returned to their seats to rejoin Frank. They were both in a state of complete ecstasy from this exhilarating experience.

"Wow! That was just great, man!" young Wesley sighed with happiness.

"Cor! Just think," Mark uttered in the same state of high elation, "we – we've actually played cricket at *Lord's!*"

"Yes, now won't that be something to tell all your friends back at school," Frank remarked..

"They'll never believe us, will they?" Wesley laughed.

"No, they'll think we're having them on," Mark added.

"You've got me as a witness though if they do, haven't you?" Frank assured them.

"Yes, and you won't forget to speak with our Headmaster about playing this Kwik-Cricket at our school, will you, Uncle?"

Frank leaned back into a comfortable position to watch the resumption of the County game once more. "No, of course I won't if you think it will do any good." He personally didn't think there would be any objections to this request. In fact, he thought it might go a long way in establishing once more this most noblest of games at their school.

Both lads sat relaxing in the sunshine, a smile spread across their faces as they watched their cricketing idols performing again.

Before close of play that evening they were privileged to see Nick Gallon score a magnificent hundred, executing an array of shots all round the Ground with utmost poise and elegance. They also witnessed the Yorkshire fast bowler take five wickets, four of which were clean bowled by him. And to top the day off, Frank managed to obtain both teams autographs for them; making their first Lord's encounter an experience never to be forgotten.

At the end of the day as they slid out of the Ground sitting in the back of Frank's car on their homeward journey, both agreed that it was positively the best day by far they'd ever had in their lives. Nothing could ever compare to this again. After all, how many other lads of their age could boast of actually playing cricket at such a prodigious Ground as Lord's? Not many, they were bound. And all on young Mark's birthday as well!

CHAPTER SEVEN

Headmaster's Decision

Turnbull sat behind the desk in his office staring at both Mark and his uncle seated opposite after having listened to them put their case for the introduction of Kwik-Cricket at Neswell Junior School.

"I give you full marks for effort concerning this venture of yours, young Adams," he addressed Mark finally. Then adjusting his spectacles to a more comfortable position on the bridge of his nose with his index finger, added: "You obviously don't give in easily, do you?"

"No, sir!" Mark replied determinedly. "At least – not where cricket is concerned, I don't."

"Be that as it may," Turnbull continued frostily, "but I do believe you are taking this whole thing far too seriously."

At this point Frank intervened. "I fully understand the lad's feelings with regards to this desire he and Wesley Jackson have in wanting to play school cricket," he spoke very eloquently on behalf of their cause.

Indeed, Mark felt honoured that his uncle had taken time out to do just this for them. Had kept his promise to talk with Turnbull on the subject. And with such haste as well, today only being the Monday following the Saturday of their unforgettable visit to Lord's. Why, he wondered, couldn't his own father be as co-operative? His response when Mark informed him of his brother's offer to help in the matter was one of disinterestedness really.

"I don't think it will do any good," was his curt reply, "but if your Uncle thinks it will help any – then good luck to him."

Why his father should be so belligerent concerning this whole business, Mark could not fathom out. After all, it wasn't as if he didn't like the sport. Far from it. He and his brother were both avid cricket lovers. Mark could well understand his present attitude if this wasn't the case. It left the youngster feeling hurt and bewildered by it all. It was almost as if his father didn't want him to play cricket for some reason. But he was determined to do so more than ever now.

In sharp contrast Wesley's father, when hearing of the youngsters plan, couldn't have been more responsive, promising to help the lads in any way he could.

"After all," Frank continued putting their case to the head, "it's a perfectly natural thing for them to want to do, isn't it? I know it was for me. How about you, Mr Turnbull – didn't you ever play cricket whilst at junior school?"

Turnbull twisted uneasily in his chair, this question from the man opposite seeming to hit upon a raw nerve inside him suddenly. He coughed nervously. "Uhmm. . . yes, well, as a matter of fact I did," he confessed. "B-but things were different then, as you are no doubt well aware of, Mr Adams."

"Yes, I realise there are changes that have taken place since those days. It doesn't necessarily mean they prove to be right though, does it?"

That's it, Uncle Frank, Mark thought. You tell the old so and so. Make him see that all we want is to form a cricket team at this school. Nothing more.

"No, it doesn't prove any such thing," Turnbull agreed with this statement. "However, you must realize that I have to go along with the education authorities decision no to include cricket in this school's sporting activities. I am powerless to do anything about it. Surely you can appreciate my position with regards to all this, Mr Adams?"

Frank leaned forward in his chair. "Of course I do, Mr Turnbull," he said to him quietly, understandingly.

Did this mean the answer was no to their hopes of a school cricket team after all then? Mark wondered to himself sadly. Surely not. Come on, Uncle Frank; don't throw our chances away now that we've come this far. Make a stand against these anti cricket people, for goodness sake.

"However. . ." Frank was obviously not going to give in that easily, much to the delight of his young nephew sitting beside him. "I do believe these youngsters in wanting a school cricket team are not asking *too* much of the authorities with their plan to achieve one. Do you, Headmaster?"

Turnbull peered at both of them over spectacles that had slid down onto the end of his rather pointed nose once again. Adjusting them to a more favourable position in which to view the pupil and his guardian, he then leaned back in his leather-clad upholstered chair to inform them of his decision.

Mark listened with bated breath for the verdict. Surely no one would prevent them from playing this safe game of Kwik-Cricket at their own school? Even old Turnbull wouldn't be *that* cruel, he thought, not daring to resume the necessary bodily function of breathing at the moment until he knew for certain whether the meeting with him had been a success or not.

The headmaster's answer seemed like an eternity in coming, while young Mark's face grew bluer and bluer the longer he held his breath waiting for it.

"No, Mr Adams," Turnbull finally addressed his uncle in a calm, deliberated tone of voice. "I honestly don't believe they are. What's more, I can't quite see anyone objecting to what they have in mind. From what you have told me, it appears that this Kwik-Cricket game can be played with a minimum amount of supervision, and I can only see good coming from it with regards to teaching the youngsters leadership and discipline, as I'm sure the education authorities will also agree when I inform them that I intend to give it the go ahead. If, as you say, this game can be set up and played off their own bat so to speak – excuse the pun – then you have my full permission to introduce it here at Neswell, gentlemen. Good luck with your venture, young Adams.

38

I'm thinking though that you will have your work cut out in forming some opposition to play against. Have you given this any thought, young man? Anyway – keep me informed of its progress, won't you?''

Both Mark and his uncle remained silent for a moment, unable to believe what they had just heard from the head. They were both of the opinion that old Turnbull was dead set against the playing of cricket at his school. Just goes to show. Even *he* can have a change of heart. Then, as they realized their plan had met with success, the pair of them smiled ecstatically at one another.

''Phew!'' Mark gasped finally with joy at hearing this wonderful news and with relief at being able to breath yet once again. He had never before in his life held his breath for such a long period of time.

''It's what you wanted to hear, isn't it?'' Frank asked him when they were outside in the corridor.

''Cor, Uncle Frank – not half! Just wait till I tell Wesley the news. Boy! He'll never believe it.''

''Be that as it may. It's as of now that the hard work starts with the forming of your cricket side, my lad.''

Yes, Mark certainly knew that; but he was confident that between them everything would be all right along those lines. The main thing was they had actually been given permission to introduce the game at his school. He couldn't have been happier with the outcome of their meeting with Turnbull. All that remained now was to find a cricket team. Mark looked forward to this challenge very much indeed.

''Right then, young Mark,'' his uncle addressed him enthusiastically. ''Tell your father I'll be around to see him this evening to discuss this school cricket business amongst the three of us. After all, this is only the first hurdle we've got over. The next is to approach Northcott Junior to see if they are interested in Kwik-Cricket. If so – then once you have got your side together – you will have a team to play against, won't you?''

''I sure will. Thanks – thanks for everything.'' Mark would never be grateful enough to his uncle for the support he had given him back there in the headmaster's office. Who knows – perhaps Mark's father might now offer some assistance with the task at hand? Well, he would soon enough find out when they all met later, wouldn't he?

For the time being, he walked tall with his uncle's friendly arm around his shoulder as they both strode proudly out of the school with smiles on their faces and feeling very pleased with themselves.

CHAPTER EIGHT

Family Get Together

True to his word, Frank arrived that evening to discuss further the business at hand with Mark and his family.

"I understand from Mark that your meeting with Turnbull was successful," his mother said to Frank in a congratulatory manner after they were all seated comfortably in the front parlour.

"Yes, he was in complete agreement with young Mark's plan once he realised it could be put into operation without having to involve any of his teachers," Frank confirmed the good news to both parents, smiling affectionately at his nephew.

Mark returned the smile, feeling very happy with life in general and grateful also to his kind uncle for having given him so much of his valuable time and support in the matter.

"So what happens now?" Mark's father seated opposite and obviously interested to know, questioned his brother.

For the first time since he had made known his desire to play school cricket, Mark thought he detected from this question that perhaps his father might possibly be showing some interest as to the outcome of his plan after all? He also observed that his father was actually without any of his usual insurance work before him on the table, which was encouraging because it meant that he might be prepared to join in with the discussion that was, after all said and done, very close to his heart really.

Mrs Adams had also observed her husband's changed attitude, which pleased her greatly, knowing that her son's interests were now being taken seriously. And if the truth were known it would do Jim good to forget about his work for a while. She looked admiringly at Mark and could see a sudden transformation in him from the innocent young boy he seemed only yesterday to that of responsible youthfulness of today. This recognition made her feel very proud to be his mother, yet at the same time sad, knowing she was losing her little boy to the beckoning outside world; but it was inevitable, as every mother is only too fully aware. She listened now in admiration to her son's confident reply to his father's question.

"Well, Dad, what happens now is that I meet with the Headmaster of Northcott Junior to see if he minds Kwik-Cricket being played there to arrange a fixture with them, that's what."

Jim Adams gazed over at his son, mulling over in his mind Mark's answer. "And what if this Headmaster *does* mind? What if he *doesn't* want cricket to be played at his school? What then?" he put to the lad aggravatingly.

Mark looked with defiance straight into his father's eyes. "Then I keep looking until I find one that will," he said with determination.

"I'm sure there'll be no objection from Northcott over it, Jim," Frank tried assuring his brother at this stage, hoping to relieve the obvious tension there was between father and son concerning this whole business. "After all, the lad's not asking for much now, is he, just to be able to play school cricket?"

Jim Adams gave his son a warm, friendly smile. "No, I suppose not," he had to confess in all honesty to his brother's statement. "I'm sorry, Mark if I appear objectionable to you on this matter. It-it's just that I don't want you getting too disappointed if things don't work out right, Son. I can see though that you've set your heart on achieving this cricketing desire, so I wish you every success with it. I only wish I could devote as much time in helping you as your uncle; but if I can assist you now in any way I will do my best to make up for lost time."

Mark heaved a great sigh of relief with this knowledge from his father. It was nice to know that there would be now no further animosity between them over this matter. ''That's nice to know,'' he said to him with a deep felt sense of gratitude.

''Of course, that goes for your mother also, Mark,'' his father gave him further family assurance of co-operation. ''In fact, I have an idea that might be of some help to your cause. Can't tell you much about it at the moment until I have the chance to check it out.''

Mark wondered what on earth his father had up his sleeve.

''I'm sure whatever it is it will be most appreciated, eh, young Mark?'' Frank said to him, a broad, knowing smile lighting up his face.

''It most certainly will,'' Mark echoed his uncle's sentiments excitedly, looking across at his father, but sensing he was being left in the dark over something by the two men.

However, his mother came to his rescue. ''That's not fair, Jim,'' she reprimanded her husband sharply. ''I think it only right you should inform Mark of your idea and not keep him in suspense. Would you agree, Frank?''

''Ohhh ... all right, Mary,'' her husband intervened good-humouredly. ''You win. I'll tell him. Won't do any harm. You see, Mark – I think I can get my company to sponsor this Kwik-Cricket idea of yours. . .''

''How do you mean, Dad?'' Mark interrupted inquisitively.

''Well ... I think I can get them to put up the money to buy enough of your Kwik-Cricket sets to supply all of the junior schools around here with.''

''*What*!'' screamed Mark in disbelief.

''Yes, it's great news all right,'' Frank agreed jubilantly, sounding just as excited as his nephew. ''Your father told me all about it last night over the phone.''

Mark was gobsmacked at hearing this. What marvellous news. It was all too good to be true really.

''If we can manage to get enough publicity from the venture to satisfy our company I am pretty sure they will go along with the idea,'' Jim Adams explained to Mark. ''Whatever – it's definitely worth a try, don't you think, Son?''

Mark sat in silence, unable to take it all in. If, as his father says, all the other schools in the district were to be kitted out with cricket gear then it might mean that they could *all* form teams just like he intended doing. Cor, he thought with glee, that's just great! There could then be an abundance of teams playing cricket within the Wufton area. It certainly was a distinct possibility. It conjured up in his mind images of youngsters like himself and Wesley participating in competitive fixtures against these other sides. A Kwik-Cricket league could be formed. It would be super.

"You definitely *will* try to persuade your firm to help us," Mark pleaded with his father. "You *will*, won't you, Dad?"

"As I said – leave it with me – and I will see what I can do," he assured the youngster.

His uncle gave Mark a friendly wink. "There – can't be fairer than that now – can you," he said warmly. "So, Mark – what do you think of the idea?"

"It's just great. Wesley will never believe me when I tell him the news."

"By the way," his mother intervened. "Where *is* young Wesley? Wasn't he supposed to be here this evening?"

Mark frowned. "He's not been well. He's not been to school today. Caught a bug or something."

"Oh, dear, I'm sorry to hear that."

"You better tell him to hurry up and get better because you'll need his help to form this team of yours, young man," Frank reminded him of the task ahead of them.

Mrs Adams rose to her feet. "Time for a cup of tea, I think," she suggested, before disappearing into the kitchen to leave the menfolk to discuss further their beloved game of cricket. She felt so relieved that her husband had decided after all to help their son with his venture. It would mean so much to Mark to have his support in this way. As, indeed it would to her also. It would hopefully help to eradicate any future tension between them brought on initially by Jim's lack of co-operation to assist their son in his desire to play cricket.

Another person who couldn't have been happier was, of course, young Mark who sat discussing with his father and his uncle the plan of action for the future as he showed them both a poster he'd made up that would be displayed on the school notice board, inviting pupils who were interested in playing cricket for Neswell to attend a trial to be held on the playing field after school bell tomorrow afternoon.

At this point, Mark's uncle informed him that he would be approaching Northcott's headmaster the following day to find out his reaction to forming a team there. And his father said he would also be contacting the man with regards to supplying this school with a Kwik-Cricket set once he got his company's go ahead to do so.

It appeared that Mark's dream was slowly but surely becoming a reality for him at long last, which made him feel very happy indeed.

CHAPTER NINE

Formation Of School Cricket Team

The response to Mark's poster at school the following day was overwhelming. Enough youngsters turned up for the trial to form at least two cricket teams. It was as well for Mark that his friend Wesley was with him initially to lend a hand. A little later, thankfully, Frank arrived on the scene to organise some order out of the somewhat chaotic attempts the youngsters were making at playing a game of cricket.

Mark knew, of course, that the number of players at any one time on the field of play should have been just the eleven representing the fielding side and the two batsmen from the opposing team. Himself and Wesley stood as umpires because they both knew of their own cricketing abilities, whereas of yet the rest of the participants were of an unknown quantity and needed to be looked at to assess their potential. Unfortunately, despite several reminders from Mark, the others took it into their heads to join in immediately. Consequently, the proceedings turned out to be somewhat of a shambles with people running about all over the place, all wanting to bowl and bat at the same time. It was at this point that Mark knew he had to establish some authority over his fellow pupils if he was to ever achieve success in forming this school cricket team of his.

"Right everyone! Listen up!" he shouted impatiently, holding the ball that he had taken from the bowler aloft in the air. "If you want to carry on with this game I suggest that all of you who are on the batting side – apart from the actual two batsmen, that is – to kindly leave the field now and go and sit down on that bench over there and wait until your name is called before venturing out here again. Otherwise we may as well pack the game up right here and now. Got that?''

This seemed to do the trick because the culprits in question began sauntering off the field, although one or two of them greeted this dressing down from Mark with disapproving mumblings.

''And anyone disobeying your captain will not be asked to participate further!'' the strict voice of Frank bellowed frighteningly at them as he emerged from behind a tree, having obviously witnessed all that was going on. Then, making sure the guilty ones involved were under control by standing menacingly behind them on the bench, added: ''Right! Carry on with your game, skipper.''

Mark was more than happy to oblige, relieved that his uncle was around to support him in the discipline of his players where this cricket trial was concerned. He looked over at his pal Wesley standing at the square leg umpire position. Wesley beamed back a broad smile at him, his white teeth glistening in the bright afternoon sunlight.

''Let's go, man!'' he urged for the trial to continue.

Mark offered the ball to the bowler at his end. ''PLAY,'' he informed the batsman.

From these humble beginnings, Mark's dream of forming a school team at Neswell began to materialize.

Between himself, Wesley and Frank, they managed to look at all the youngsters who came to attend the trial. In the two hours it took to do this they were able to establish those who were the potential cricketers among them that then finally left them with a list of players from which to form a well-balanced side. The team consisted mainly of Indian and Pakistan youngsters, while the rest was of West Indian and English origin.

''You know – you two will do more for race relations here in Wufton than any of our so called politicians,'' Frank said to both

Mark and Wesley later when they were sitting in Mark's parents house discussing the events of the past couple of hours.

"There were some good cricketers among them though," Mark commented, guzzling a cold glass of orange that his mother had made up for him and Wesley as reward for their efforts. They were absolutely dying of thirst.

"T'rific!" young Wesley agreed with his colleague enthusiastically. "Man – those Patel brothers certainly know how to bat and bowl, that's for sure."

"Your coloured friend, Williams – he looks a good fast bowling prospect, Wes?" Frank stated knowledgeably.

"You'll have to watch you don't lose your place to him," Mark joked with his friend, then added in a more serious tone of voice: "I noticed you limping today when you were bowling. Nothing wrong, is there?"

Wesley rubbed his right leg vigorously. "Just a bit stiff, that's all."

Mrs Adams entered the room with more drinks for everyone.

"So, the cricket trial went all right then, Mark?" his father enquired after they were all settled with their refreshments.

"Yes, it went very well, thank you, Dad. We had a great turn out for it. Uncle Frank and Wes helped out as well. We hope to organise a proper match tomorrow afternoon with the players we picked."

His father then offered him a friendly smile, knowing that what he was about to say would please him very much. "Well. . ." he began slowly, "you will be pleased to know that my company have okayed your Kwik- Cricket kits for six local schools if they request them. What do you think to that . . .?"

"Wow! That's just great, man!" Wesley uttered with excitement at hearing this news.

Mark was in a state of sheer ecstasy. He felt happier than he had ever felt in his life before as his father's announcement registered fully with him. It definitely now looked like his school cricket dream was well on its way to becoming a reality.

"That-that's just marvellous, Dad," he thanked his father, a huge smile lighting up his young face. "It's just what is wanted to get this thing off the ground."

"I thought it might please you, Son. Now it's down to you to make it work."

His father seemed very excited over this cricket issue, and, if the truth were really known, was hopefully looking forward to its success as much as Mark. His insurance company had agreed to become sponsors and put up the money for the equipment needed by the schools for the project. In return, they obviously expected as much publicity for themselves as possible from the venture. Hopefully, then everyone would be happy, especially his son. Jim was glad now to be lending a hand in this way, even though he knew he couldn't devote as much time as his brother Frank to the cause. Nevertheless, he was sure his help would be of great value in the long run. It would be a team effort. A family one at that, he thought with pride, smiling across at his wife as he caught her eye.

Indeed, Mary was more than pleased at the way things were progressing and couldn't hide the happiness she felt for her son. The tension that had prevailed these past few weeks among the family was now no more and they were now working together harmoniously because of Jim's participation with their son's project. She felt an enormous sense of pride for the both of them.

"Now that you've all had your say in the matter," Frank intervened at this stage, "*I* have some news that might interest you, young Mark."

Mark could hardly conceal his excitement at the prospect of another possibility toward furthering his aim being hinted at. "What news, Uncle Frank? Oh, what news?"

"Your uncle's going to take us to Lord's, that's what!" young Wesley exclaimed, anticipating the likelihood of this happening again, the memory of their last visit still vivid in his mind. Who knows – perhaps maybe even another chance to play cricket there as well? Wesley still couldn't get over the fact of actually having been allowed this remarkable opportunity to do so in the first place. Neither could his father, who was absolutely flabbergasted after being told of this achievement by him. However, no further invitation was on offer now, as he was about to discover.

"I paid Northwick School a visit earlier. . ." Frank began; but was prevented from continuing further by the intervention of his over zealous nephew with a barrage of questions.

"Did you. . . ? What did they say. . . ? Are they interested in playing cricket, Uncle Frank, are they. . . ? What did the Headmaster say. . . ?"

Mark's uncle took a deep breath before replying to this cross-examination. "Yes, Mark, they *are* interested in playing cricket, and the Headmaster *is* keen to allow a team to be formed. Providing there is someone to organise and run it, that is."

"And what did you say – what did you tell him, Uncle Frank?"

"I told him that *you* would be looking after things here at Neswell, Mark, and that *I* would take charge at Northwick with the aim of forming a school cricket team there."

Mark stared at his uncle in disbelief. "You told him *what*?" he gasped finally as the reality of this statement dawned on him. What he was hearing was all too good to be true. Things could hardly get better.

"I think what Uncle Frank is saying is that he is prepared to help form some opposition to play against your school side, Mark," his father clarified his brother's position for him.

Mark knew this, but it was just taking a little while to sink in, that was all.

"Man! That's great news," young Wesley, beaming with excitement, spoke for everyone.

"It most certainly is," Mark's mother agreed happily. In fact, she couldn't have been happier for her son at that precise moment.

It was at this precise moment also that Wesley made quite a profound statement. "My Dad says he'll teach cricket to the kids down at Cannon School and form a team there as well if they want."

The lad's utterances fell on deaf ears to begin with. But – like all the other previous offers of help that evening – was then met with sheer jubilation by everyone.

"At this rate there will be more fixtures than you'll know what to do with, eh, Mark?" his father jested.

"Especially if they all require teas." His mother contemplated the thought of this possibility.

It was left to Mark's uncle to put things in their right perspective though. "I'm sure our team manager here is quite capable of handling everything to the best of his ability, aren't you, Mark?" he said to him.

"You bet I can," Mark answered with strong determination. "Just give us the chance, eh, Wes, we'll show 'em, won't we?"

"We sure will," his second in command acknowledged with equal determination.

"It's certainly nice to know that your father is keen to assist in this way, Wesley," Frank thanked the lad profusely. "I'm sure his input will be most valuable. Please tell him I'll get in touch to discuss this further, won't you?"

"I sure will Unc. . . I mean, Mr Adams," the West Indian boy hurriedly corrected himself from addressing Frank as uncle. Somehow though, it seemed very natural for him to do so because of his close involvement with the school now.

Frank gave the lad a warm smile, feeling quite touched really with the boy's friendliness and obvious trust toward him. He felt, along with his nephew, that they were now beginning to work together as a team.

Others in the family were of the same opinion also as broad grins appeared on their faces as their feelings of affection for this youngster became apparent. There was also a genuine mood of cooperativeness amongst them all and of a team spirit and determination to set into motion Mark's plan.

"If Uncle Frank *was* also your uncle, then I suppose us two would be brothers, wouldn't we?" Mark joked with his school pal laughingly.

"Yes, Wesley – and it would also mean that Mary and myself would be your parents," Mark's father added in good humour.

The fact of the matter, however, was that the two boys were each other's best friend really and would not have minded in the least if they did happen to be brothers. That way, they would have been even better friends than they already were. Leastways – that's how they both felt.

"Be that as it may," Frank addressed the pair of them in a more serious tone of voice. "You know that you will need to work hard together if you want this cricket project to succeed, don't you?"

"Yes – and we intend to do just that, don't we, skipper?" Wesley replied positively, looking across at his comrade.

"Indeed we do," Mark gave this assurance to his vice captain.

"I'm glad to hear it, because a great deal lies ahead of you from now on."

With that, Mary collected the empty cups and disappeared into the kitchen to brew more tea for the Kwik-Cricket committee members.

The meeting went on until well past ten-o-clock. Matters that came under discussion were: the need for future umpires to be present at matches once arranged. Also the need for scorers to record details of all these games. Other important issues debated covered those of the actual facilities required, i.e. cricket pitches and preparation of them. Changing room accommodation for the teams. Whether teas and refreshments would be required. The start times for these games.

The senior gentlemen even talked about the possibility of arranging an opening ceremony for the first match and of approaching some professional cricketing personalities to be present along with press coverage of the event.

To the two youngsters it all sounded very exciting, especially as both were actually responsible for starting the project to begin with. And none more so than Mark, the original instigator of the whole concept. But, like his uncle had emphasised earlier, he knew that there was still a long way to go and a lot of hard work involved for this dream of his to become reality.

CHAPTER TEN

Media Attention

It took just two weeks by those concerned to arrange the first Kwik-Cricket fixture between the Neswell and Northcott Junior Schools in Wufton, the game itself to be played on a Saturday morning on the playing field at Neswell. Yes, a fortnight, during which time young Mark and his father, his uncle, Wesley and his father, somehow managed between them through sheer hard work and determination to accomplish this wonderful achievement.

Mark and Wesley took charge of their school team, sifting through the eligible players from the practise match list to finally come up with what they considered to be the strongest representative eleven.

The opposing side was organised by the grown ups – namely – Frank and Julian, and were assured by both men that they were most impressed with the cricketing talent that went into the making of this side.

Later in the week, Mark's uncle took him to meet Mr Grimbald, the headmaster at Northcott.

"So you're the young lad who has created all this interest in cricket, are you?" the man welcomed him with a smile.

"The one and only," Frank proudly introduced him.

The three of them sat and talked for almost an hour about the forthcoming cricket match, at the end of which Grimbald wished Mark's venture all the success in the world. He then went on to tell him that if there was any more he could do to help, he would be only too pleased to lend his assistance. He also assured him that his school's facilities would be at Neswell's disposal on the return fixture, and that his PE teacher was interested to stand as umpire, and his secretary, as scorer for the match. Good news indeed for young Mark.

Arrangements for this opening game had all been taken care of, old Turnbull having been most cooperative in the matter by also giving permission for cricket to be played at his school on any Saturday morning throughout the summer with the use also of the Staff Room for changing.

The match umpires would be Frank and Wesley's father. Mark's mother would organise food and tea to be taken between innings in the gymnasium. Another interesting aspect was that Frank had actually persuaded the head groundsman at Lord's to travel down on the day to cut and prepare a wicket for the big occasion. He was also working on the Middlesex captain and his team to come along to be present at the match, the County not having a fixture on that particular day. There was rumour also that Trevor Sinclair, the BBC cricket commentator, was showing an interest in this special occasion and would possibly be making an appearance.

To young Mark all these happenings seemed so unbelievable. He couldn't have been happier at the way things were progressing. With this enthusiasm from all concerned it proved to him that the game of cricket at junior school level desperately needed to be re-introduced – not only here in Wufton – but throughout all of the schools in the United Kingdom as a vehicle to make the educational authorities sit up and take action to put right the appalling situation that was denying youngsters the opportunity to participate in this most noblest of games. For the time being, however, the game would be just confined to the two schools in question.

After talking to Frank, Wesley's father said that he would be only too happy to help establish another school cricket team down the road at Cannon Junior, and would make a start as soon possible on this project. Mark thought that perhaps after this first Neswell game maybe other schools in the area might take up the offer of the Kwik-Cricket kits from his father's company? He sincerely hoped they would, for then a fixture list could be drawn up that would enable them to play cricket every Saturday morning throughout the season amongst each other.

The first inclination Mark had that the press had got wind of his cricketing endeavours was one evening after arriving home from school a week before the first actual match to find a reporter from the local paper sitting in his living room.

"This is Mike Kelly from the Wufton Gazette, Mark," his mother informed him. "He says that he is very interested in writing an article for his paper on your fight for school cricket. He wants to know if you have any objections to this?"

Objections? Of course he didn't. He could do with as much publicity as possible, and it would certainly help his cause.

His mother, feeling more proud each day of her son, left the pair to discuss the subject and went to make some tea. A newspaper reporter indeed! What next? she wondered. And her Mark only just eleven years of age. Wait till his father hears of this.

In fact, this coverage proved to be somewhat beneficial to his father's company with the publicity gained from it as the actual article mentioned that it was them who were supplying the cricket equipment for the match in question and for other schools in the future if required. The report covered all aspects of Mark and his family and friends involvement in bringing about his burning desire to play school cricket in Wufton. It also included a photo of Mark taken outside his front door after the interview. Who would have thought a few weeks back that his picture would be in the local paper regarding this? It was all unbelievable really.

One thing to emerge from it at the moment that did bother Mark somewhat though was concern for his friend, Wesley, and his reaction to all this publicity as there was no mention made of him in the article. This was a pity, because Mark pointed out to the reporter the fact that the forming of the school cricket team had been a joint venture between the two of them. Would Wesley now be jealous of Mark because of all this attention suddenly bestowed on him? Would the two of them fall out over it? This was the last thing Mark wanted to happen. No, Wesley was as much a part of this whole business as he was and he wanted his friend to receive the same amount of praise and publicity. After all, he couldn't afford to upset his fast bowler. It might affect his performance on the cricket field. And Mark needed a hundred per cent effort from his colleague. Perhaps he should have a word with someone about his concern to see if Wesley could somehow be included in another newspaper article in recognition of his work?

The following day it was Frank who came to the rescue yet once again by managing to arrange an interview for young Mark and Wesley with the cricket correspondent of the *Daily Globe*, Peter Blakewell. He was an old friend of Frank's. After hearing the plight of the youngsters and of what they were trying to accomplish, he became only too eager to make known their story in his newspaper to the nation's readers. The writer's poignant article described every aspect of the present set up with the junior schools in Wufton and of the complete absence of cricket in them and was given a whole page coverage in the *Globe* a few days later with a marvellous picture of the two boys in question posing arm in arm together on the sports field of their school with the headline caption:

YOUNGSTERS TAKE ON AUTHORITIES
IN BID FOR RETURN OF SCHOOL CRICKET.

If anyone had told Mark that his quest for cricket would make sporting headlines in a prominent national newspaper, he would never have believed them. Deep down though both he and Wesley were overjoyed with this supportive turn of events. As were indeed their families, and, of course, all those involved at Neswell and Northcott junior schools. To say that Mark and Wesley was the centre of attention in their hometown and at school would certainly be an understatement. And being in the limelight like this led to further publicity for the pair of them that following week.

A team from the BBC Radio 4 crew visited their school to interview them and their headmaster for a news programme to be heard by thousands of listeners at six-o-clock that evening. Mark was a little worried that Turnbull might not take too kindly to this exercise; frightened he might change his mind about letting them play cricket at Newswell after all. However, his fears along these lines proved to be unfounded because Turnbull cooperated fully with these people to everything they requested. And even more so when later that afternoon a team of television personnel arrived on the scene to record further interviews with him and his newsworthy pupils for the programme *Out And About* to be screened to the nation following the six-o-clock news that night. In fact, the head appeared to revel in his television debut and came across as someone very understanding to the needs of these youngsters, and indeed to all fellow pupils in and around the town of Wufton who were in the same predicament as Neswell with the absence of cricket in their schools.

Turnbull did emphasise the fact that this present situation was not one of his making, but that of the education authorities, and until they had a rethink in this matter he would have to go along with them in their present line of thought.

"But I have no objections with two of my pupils introducing Kwik-Cricket at our school providing they are willing to undertake the supervision of this game," Turnbull informed the television interviewer categorically. "And this – I am glad to say – they have done admirably well by incorporating their parents, relatives and friends to help them with their plan. Therefore, I can see no reason whatsoever why they should be denied the full use of our school's playing facilities, and I wish them every success with it."

It was now time for the youngsters to explain their side of the story to the TV presenter. The pair handled the experience very well indeed considering how awe inspiring it was for them. Mark, as the main instigator for believing he could form a school cricket team to begin with, and Wesley as his co-worker and vice skipper, answered questions and expressed their views in a most articulate manner indeed.

The two boys had now become the centre of attraction at school due to their appearances on television and radio. This created numerous discussions amongst their fellow pupils and members of staff, some of whom were in favour of what they hoped to achieve, while others, on the other hand, appeared to be dead set against the idea altogether.

"You have to hand it to those boys," Turnbull complimented the two cricketing heroes in the Staff Room during coffee break later that week. "They certainly show character in all of this."

"In *my* opinion I think it is all a great deal of fuss over nothing," the boy's teacher, Mr Fox, contradicted the headmaster's praise dismissively.

Turnbull shot this member of staff a disapproving look from his seated position opposite. "You are perfectly entitled to your personal view, of course, Mr Fox," he addressed the man sharply, "but I do think you will find that the general census of opinion among the majority over this issue is of an overwhelming support for the initiative these two lads have shown in fighting for something that they really believe in. The interest they've aroused within the press and television media has been rather extraordinary indeed. Would you not agree?"

"Be that as it may, Mr Turnbull, but I still firmly believe that more attention should be concentrated on their education rather than attracting all this hype over whether or not they are allowed to play cricket at this school. After all, surely what they are here for is to learn, isn't it?"

Turnbull was becoming somewhat agitated with these comments from the teacher. "Well, of *course* that is why our pupils come to school, man!" he snapped at Fox angrily. "Nobody is denying that. But I think you will find that throughout the history of English schools there has *always* been cricket played in them up until this recent decision by the so called authorities not to any more."

"A decision no doubt that must have been thoroughly thought through before being finally arrived at," Fox added sarcastically.

The headmaster finished drinking his coffee, and then slowly rose to his feet. "Until quite recently I confess to having thoughts similar to yours concerning this cricket business, Mr Fox. But after deliberating somewhat on the issue upon hearing the case put forward by young master Adams for the re-introduction of the sport in the junior schools of Wufton, I have changed my mind and am now thoroughly convinced that what this boy is fighting for is right. There *should* be cricket played in them, Mr Fox. I believe the authorities are wrong in not allowing it, and in the future I shall do everything within my power to persuade them otherwise."

Prior to closing the door after him on his way out of the Staff Room, Turnbull swung round to look his fellow teacher straight in the eye, declaring to him with all the authority at his disposal as the head of school: "I notice you do not take the same line with the school's football team, Mr Fox? How many games did you organise for them last season, may I ask. . . ?"

Fox declined to answer this rather leading question from the headmaster, hiding, almost behind his coffee cup in the hope of avoiding further outbursts from his superior. He had never seen Mr Turnbull so irate before. The football statement aimed personally at him brought home the fact of his hypocrisy concerning school sports in general. After all, he had no qualms whatsoever about Neswell running a soccer team now, had he? The truth of the matter was he just couldn't stand the game of cricket in any shape or form. God forbid it should ever be played at this school again along the lines that old Turnbull was now advocating, he thought with horror.

"Under the circumstances, I'm sure you won't mind if I put your name forward to umpire Neswell's cricket team if they are allowed to have one in the future, Mr Fox?" the headmaster addressed this member of staff whom he found to be most pompous in his attitude toward cricket.

The teacher in question made no reply to the request being

asked of him; but just sat there giving his headmaster a disapproving look as he went out through the door.

Turnbull, however, was feeling quite pleased with himself for having had this outburst with Fox. The man had long been needing a dressing down of this nature. And to think it had ultimately been brought on by the actions of one single minded pupil from his school. Yes, young Adams was certainly becoming answerable for quite a number of things that were happening at Neswell at the present moment, that's for sure. Not least, for all the publicity it had attracted over the past week, and, no doubt, even more with the advent of the Kwik-Cricket match this weekend against Northcott. But as far as he was concerned it was all good publicity that would benefit the school in the long run. Yes, the young Adams lad was to be highly commended for showing so much initiative in his desire to play cricket, especially as he as headmaster at Neswell Junior had given him so little encouragement in the past. His only wish now was for those in authority to be converted in the same manner as he with the idea.

CHAPTER ELEVEN

Concern for Wesley

What with the press, radio and television coverage that Mark and Wesley had attracted, both boys were delighted at the way things had progressed for them. None more so than young Mark, especially now that his closest friend had also gained recognition for his part in bringing their dream to fruition. Not to forget his uncle, and, indeed, his father and mother and the active rolls they were all playing in this also. And, of course, Wesley's own father's assistance in gaining them an opposing side to play against on Saturday.

So, it was arranged that they should all meet that Thursday night round at Mark's house to watch the television interview recorded earlier that day with the two boy heroes. They would also discuss tactics concerning their very first cricket fixture.

"I wonder what we'll look like on tele?" Wesley beamed jubilantly as the pair ambled out of the school gates on their homeward journey.

"I can hardly wait to find out, can you?" Mark replied excitedly, skipping along on the grass verge.

Wesley joined his friend in this exercise. "Bet ol' Foxy won't think much to it."

"I bet. We certainly foxed him all right, didn't we, Wes?"

"Yeah, didn't we."

The two of them skipped merrily along, both full of the joys of living for having brought about their dream of cricket, both shrieking with delight at this achievement.

It was at this moment that young Wesley suddenly let out a piercing scream and tumbled over on the grass holding tight to his leg. "*Jeeze!*" he hollowed, obviously in much pain.

Mark came to an abrupt halt in front of his friend. "What's the matter, Wes? What on earth have you done?" he asked with alarm.

"I-I dunno. I think I've twisted my knee."

Mark gazed worriedly down at his friend. "Can you stand on it?"

"I dunno. . . I'll try. It sure does hurt though."

Mark bent down and took hold of his friend's arm and placed it round his neck, then gently helped him to his feet.

Wesley rested himself in this position for a while to regain his composure.

"How does it feel now?" Mark enquired, supporting Wesley's body in an upright position.

His friend slowly lowered his weight onto his painful leg. "I-I think it's okay," he muttered, but limping as he tried to walk with Mark's help.

"Nothing's broke, I don't think," Mark tried reassuring him. "You've probably just twisted it."

Wesley tried managing a few hazardous steps on his own. "Yeah – it don't feel too bad. *Jeeze!* How on earth did I manage to fall like that?"

"You slipped on the grass, that's how, Wes."

"Yeah, I suppose I did. Anyway – it feels quite a lot better now."

Wesley succeeded in continuing to walk unaided on their homeward journey together.

"You sure you're all right, Wes? Only we don't want you crocked for Saturday's match, do we?"

"No – honest – I'm fine, honest," his friend insisted. "I wouldn't miss that match for the world, would I?"

They came to a halt at the end of the road where Wesley lived.

"And you'll be okay to watch TV later round my house?" Mark asked his pal for this assurance.

"Course I will. Don't wanna miss *that* either, do I?" Wesley guaranteed with a broad smile on his face.

"Good. Well, I'll see you later then, Wes?"

"Yeah, I'll see you later, Mark."

Mark watched his friend limp along the road and disappear inside his house. What a carry on, he thought. Only a day or so to go before the first cricket match at their school, and here was his opening bowler in danger of nearly of missing it because of a silly accident. Still, the main thing was that Wesley had sustained no serious injury because of it.

CHAPTER TWELVE

Hospitalisation for Wesley

Ten minutes before the *Out And About* TV coverage of the Kwik-Cricket story was due to commence in the Adams household that night, a telephone message from Wesley's father with the news that he was taking his son to hospital for an X-ray on his leg was received by Mr Adams.

"It appears that young Wesley's twisted his knee and is on his way to the hospital," Mr Adams informed everyone of this unfortunate state of affairs. "Do you know anything about this, Mark?"

"He did slip on the grass verge coming home from school this afternoon," Mark explained, frowning. "He seemed to be all right though. Gosh! I hope it's nothing serious?"

"Probably just a precaution taken by the boy's father to make sure he's all right," Frank tried reassuring his nephew.

"The lad's in some considerable pain apparently," Mr Adams added with some concern.

"Poor Wesley," Mrs Adams sighed unhappily.

They all sat in silence for a while, each with there own private thoughts.

What if Wesley had caused himself an injury? Mark contemplated with a certain amount of trepidation. Would it mean him missing the cricket match on Saturday after all? What bad luck this would be for his pal if true. And all because of that silly tumble this afternoon.

"If it proves to be serious, it might mean you having to find a replacement bowler for your match on Saturday, Mark?'' his father, obviously sympathetic toward Wesley if the lad had to drop out, yet facing up to the consequences it might have on the school eleven.

"I'm sure he has someone in mind for just such an eventuality, haven't you, Mark?'' Frank enquired sensitively, knowing full well how upset his nephew would be concerning the welfare of his school friend.

"I do have another bowler lined up in an emergency, yes,'' Mark answered quietly, but hoped secretly that he wouldn't have to call upon his services. ''Perhaps they will find nothing wrong with Wes, eh, Uncle Frank?''

Frank looked across at his brother, knowing Mark needed some reassurance that his friend was indeed all right; but felt this would be better coming from his father rather than he on this occasion.

"That's right, Son,'' said Jim Adams, as if reading his brother's thoughts. ''They'll probably discover nothing wrong with your friend Wesley other than a minor sprain of his ankle. No doubt he'll be as right as rain come Saturday – you'll see.''

Mark, seated opposite, held his father's gaze. ''Do you really think so, Dad?'' he asked, managing a smile.

"I agree,'' his uncle added. ''Julian will more than likely phone to verify this shortly, Mark.''

"In the meantime there's your television programme to watch, isn't there?'' Mrs Adams reminded everyone.

Young Mark had suddenly no interest to view this now that his best pal wasn't there to share the experience with him. It just wouldn't be the same without him somehow. And particularly not after all they had accomplished together these past few weeks.

"I don't want to watch it,'' he sulked.

"Oh, don't be silly, Mark,'' his mother scolded him light-heartedly. ''Of course you do.''

Suddenly, a thought entered his head. ''Do you think . . .

would you mind taking me to the hospital, Dad, so as I can see my friend?''

His father looked at his brother and his wife in turn, realizing that if he refused this request he would be causing Mark a great deal of worry until he knew for certain that Wesley was all right. ''Yes, if that's what you really want, Son,'' he agreed, rising to his feet.

''But what about the TV programme?'' asked Mrs Adams. ''It would be such a shame to miss it after all your hard work.''

''I much prefer to go see Wesley,'' Mark informed his mother before standing to join his father.

''I must say I admire your sense of loyalty to your friend, Mark,'' his uncle commented, giving him a friendly smile.

''And so do I, Son,'' his father added with pride.

His mother, knowing that the TV business was of no importance now that the youngsters concerned had achieved what they had set out to do, turned to Frank and said: ''I'll make a cup of tea and we can chat about arrangements for the Saturday game.''

''I'm sure we won't be too long,'' Jim Adams stated, leaving the room with Mark.

The hospital was only ten minutes drive away, and Mark's father soon located Wesley and his father sitting in Out Patients on the ground floor.

Mark immediately ran to his friend's side. ''How are you, Wes?'' he enquired, sitting down beside him.

''I think I'm okay, Mark,'' Wesley said, offering him a broad smile. ''They've X-rayed me knee. We're waiting to see the Doctor now.''

Mr Adams looked down at the young patient. ''What have *you* been up to then, young fella?''

''I slipped on the grass verge at school, Mr Adams and hurt my leg. I'm sure it's nothing serious. It *does* hurt though.''

''That's why I thought it best to bring him to the hospital,'' Wesley's father told them seriously. ''You never know – there *could* be something wrong after his fall.''

''Very sensible of you, if I may say so,'' Mr Adams agreed.

"You will be all right to play on Saturday, won't you, Wes?" Mark asked his pal anxiously.

"Yeah, I should think so," Wesley replied with conviction. "I'm *sure* I'll be okay by then."

At this stage Wesley's father interrupted their conversation. "We'll listen to what the Doctor has to say first before making any hasty decisions about playing cricket, shall we, Son?"

As Mark sat looking at Wesley he realized how much his pal meant to him, and recalled the very first time they had befriended each other on their opening day at Neswell four years ago. They had hit it off together from the start, both of them sharing the same interests, especially the love of cricket. And of course their families interest in the sport also. During those years this friendship had developed into one of closeness and loyalty between them. Just the thought that Wesley might now have to miss the very first cricket match at Neswell this coming Saturday because of injury filled young Mark with utter dismay. He just could not visualize playing the game without his chum in the side. It would be so unfair if he couldn't after all the effort they had put into bringing this day to fruition. It meant so much to them. Just as playing at Lord's the other week had.

Young Wesley, sensing his friend's melancholy thoughts, tried cheering him up by saying: "Did you see us on the tele earlier, Mark?"

"No – we left just as it was about to start," Mark sighed pensively.

"We saw it, didn't we, Dad? We watched it in the Ward opposite while waiting for a Doctor. I thought we came across quite well."

Julian, who had been talking to Mr Adams, smiled across at his son. "Yes, you most certainly did. Quite the television personalities now you two, aren't we?" He gave a chuckle.

"Who'd have thought we would find ourselves on television, eh, captain?" Wesley put to his friend with great pride, knowing that he indeed did have a true friend in Mark for having forsaken a chance to see himself on TV to come and visit him in hospital.

Mark moved closer to his vice skipper. "I *do* hope they find nothing wrong, Wes," he spoke softly to him with deep sincerity. " 'Cos if they do and it means you can't play on Saturday, then I don't think *I* would want to either."

His friend gave him a long, hard look with his dark brown eyes. "Don't talk so silly, man! Of *course* you must play. You're the skipper, ain't you? Don't let me hear you talk like that again, even if I *do* have to miss the match. And don't let our folks hear you talk like it either, man – cos they won't like what you're sayin'. You understand?"

Mark knew in his heart his pal was speaking the truth. "Yeah, I understand, Wes," he replied. "Its just that. . .well, I shall miss you not being in the team, that's all."

His companion gave him another long stare. "An' don't you think *I* won't miss playing? Don't you see that you jus' gotta play, man, for the sake of everything we worked for? For the sake of the team an' the school an' everybody?"

At this point the doctor appeared on the scene from behind a screen. "May I have a word with you, Mr Jackson." He peered down at Wesley over his half-moon reading spectacles before disappearing behind the screen with Julian.

Mr Adams came over to join the two boys. "How are you urchins getting on then?" he joked with them, endeavouring to relieve the tension that Wesley was undoubtedly feeling at the doctor's request to talk to his father about his condition.

"We're okay, thanks," Mark answered, the tone of his voice however betraying his obvious concern for Wesley's welfare.

Wesley's attitude to the whole business though in sharp contrast was one of nonchalance really. "Well . . ." he began, a huge smile lighting up his mischievous face. "If they *do* happen to find something wrong, then they'll just have to put it right, won't they?"

"Of course they will, Wesley," Mr Adams agreed with the boy. "Of course they will."

Mark though, unable to conceal his anxiety for his chum, was secretly dreading the doctor's findings. "Perhaps they *won't* find anything wrong with you, Wes?" he uttered hopefully.

At which point the doctor and Julian emerged from behind the screen.

"What's the verdict, Pa?" Wesley asked his father outright.

The doctor allowed the father to explain the position regarding his son.

"They want you to stay in hospital for further tests," he told Wesley truthfully. "Doctor Dudley wishes to confer with another colleague about your case. Unfortunately *he* won't be on duty till the early hours of the morning. . ."

"So what is wrong with Wesley, Mr Jackson?" Mark asked his friend's father impatiently, unable to hide his concern.

The doctor cleared his throat. "To be perfectly honest we're not absolutely certain at this stage, lad," he began hesitantly. "The X-ray showed no bones to be broken. . ."

"So what's the problem – what *is* wrong with him?" Mark interrupted, looking at the doctor, then at Mr Jackson for an explanation.

The doctor removed his spectacles. "Let's just say that I am not *too* happy with certain areas of your X-ray," he addressed Wesley. "I want Doctor Mitchell to examine you first thing in the morning and that's why I would like you to stay in overnight. It will save us all a great deal of time this way."

"I see," said Wesley rather despondently, then added: "Does this mean I can't play cricket on Saturday?"

Dr Dudley offered Wesley a warm smile. "I'm afraid I can't say at this stage, young man. We will know more tomorrow after running further tests. Okay?"

Wesley sighed unhappily. "Yeah, I suppose so."

"I'll leave you to talk things over with your father and friend while I make arrangements to admit you to one of our Wards."

After the doctor departed there was a prolonged silence between the saddened and stunned persons gathered round young Wesley.

69

"What does it *all* mean, Dad?" Mark sought for an explanation concerning the welfare of his best friend.

"It means they don't want to discharge Wesley tonight only to have to bring him back again in the morning for a further consultation," Mr Jackson explained to the youngsters in a calm manner, trying to eradicate any cause for alarm they might be feeling.

"Yes, I'm sure there's nothing for you to worry yourselves over," Mr Adams added with a friendly smile for their benefit.

A young, dark-haired nurse entered the room. "If you would like to come this way, please," she beckoned Mr Adams and Wesley.

Wesley struggled to his feet with help from his father. It was at this stage that Mark knew there was something more seriously wrong with his friend's condition than was first suspected.

"I-I'll be seeing you then, Wes?" he stammered emotionally, his bright eyes filling up with tears. "Take care now. . .I'll pop in tomorrow to see how you are."

Julian helped his son into the wheelchair the nurse was holding for him.

"Sure thing, man!" Wesley answered bravely, glancing back over his shoulder as the nurse wheeled him up the corridor.

"Bye, Wesley!" Mr Adams shouted after him with affection.

On their homeward journey very few words were exchanged between Mark and his father. Both were now very worried indeed about the outcome of Wesley's condition.

Back at the house Mark's mother and uncle were most upset to hear of Wesley's hospitalisation and hoped the outcome of it all would not prove to be too serious for the lad.

"What a shame if he has to miss the match on Saturday?" Mrs Adams questioned this possibility sorrowfully.

"Yes, a crying shame," Frank agreed with a worried frown.

Young Mark couldn't bear the thought of this eventuality. Then he remembered Wesley's words to him back at the hospital and he knew that come what may he would just have to lead the

Neswell School Cricket Team out onto the field of play this coming Saturday with or without his pal.

"Perhaps Wes might be allowed to watch the match even if he can't play?" Mark put to his family hopefully.

"Yes, perhaps he might at that," his mother agreed sympathetically.

His father and uncle both looked at him thoughtfully for a moment.

"Who knows . . .?" his father contemplated the idea.

"I'm sure if it is at all possible then the Doctor will allow it, Mark," his uncle commented. "But *your* main objective now *must* be with the cricket. You have to try and put young Wesley's injury out of your mind. He will soon bounce back, you'll see."

"Oh, and while we are on the subject, Mark," his mother added with a warm smile, "Nick Gallon phoned while you were at the hospital. . ."

"Yes, and he asked to speak to *you* personally," Frank intervened, unable to hide his excitement that the Middlesex captain should contact his nephew in this manner.

If anything was to stop him worrying about his friend it was certainly this piece of information. "Nick Gallon phoned *here*?" he gasped in disbelief.

"Yes, I couldn't believe it when he told me his name," his mother continued excitedly.

"Your mother got herself in such a tizz. . .Didn't know what to say to him, did she . . .?"

Mark couldn't believe it. After all, its not every day that the captain of a County Cricket Club rings you, is it?

"What did he have to say, Uncle Frank? What did he want?"

"Oh, that he would be bringing along most of his team to watch your first Kwik-Cricket match on Saturday. Also, that he was sorry to hear of Wesley's injury and hoped he would recover in time to play. He finally wished you every success with your venture, and said that you were doing the game of cricket proud by getting it back into the schools in this area."

"*Cor!*" exclaimed Mark in awe. "He actually said *all* that?"

"Now *won't* that be something to tell all your mates at school?" his father said, obviously feeling very proud of him.

Mark couldn't quite take it all in really. If anyone had said a week ago that this would be happening to him he would have thought them silly. But the reality was that it was happening.

Before going to bed that night, both his father and uncle congratulated him on his fine achievements. He knew though that he couldn't have come this far with his dream without the help of all those concerned who had joined forces with him to make it become a reality. He was thinking especially of Wesley, and could only hope and pray that he would be fit enough to play Saturday.

CHAPTER THIRTEEN

Headmaster's Devastating News

The first inclination Mark had that things were not as they should be was the following day when the headmaster entered his classroom with a sullen look on his face.

"Would you come and see me right away, please, Adams," Turnbull said to him quietly before heading off in the direction of his office.

"Yes, sir!" answered Mark obediently. Numerous thoughts flashed through his mind as to why the head should want to see him. Surely, he thought, nothing could go wrong with the cricket match as this stage? Maybe the authorities had changed their mind about giving permission to stage it at Neswell after all? A negative thought indeed from the youngster, but until the very first ball was bowled on Saturday, only then would he be absolutely convinced it would be allowed.

"You better run along," old Foxey advised him from behind his desk in front of the blackboard.

"Do you know why he wants to see me, sir?" Mark asked the teacher on his way out.

"No, I'm afraid I don't, Adams."

Mr Foxwell, as if reading the boy's thoughts with regards to his precious sport, added: "Don't worry, I'm sure it has nothing to do with your cricket match, young man."

"Maybe the television people want to see you again, Mark!" a voice from the back of the classroom suggested as he went out.

He knocked on the door of Turnbull's office.

"Come in!" said the headmaster's voice.

"Please sit down."

Turnbull sat at his desk gazing in front of him. "I'm afraid, Mark, that I have some rather bad news for you," he said to him sternly. "There's no real way of telling you this, so I won't beat about the bush and come straight to the point. It concerns your young friend. The hospital have just informed me that they have had to operate and amputate Wesley's leg from above the knee after detecting a cancerous tumour. I-I'm so sorry to have to be the one to tell you this, Mark."

Mark looked at the headmaster in total disbelief at this devastating news. "They did *what*!" he gasped.

"I know – it's tragic – truly tragic. I can't believe it myself."

"But ... No, they can't have. They ... *No*! Oh, Wes. *No* ... !"

It was all too much for Mark and he burst into tears. "I-I'm sorry, sir!" he sobbed uncontrollably. "It...It's just..."

Turnbull got to his feet and made his way round to comfort Mark, placing a hand on his shoulder. "That's it, lad – let it out – you go straight ahead and cry. I-I'll leave you to be on your own. When you feel all right you take yourself off home and we will see you tomorrow at the cricket match."

The headmaster took an envelope from his pocket and handed it to Mark. "Wesley's Father had this delivered to the school for you earlier," he said to him, before departing quietly.

Mark couldn't remember how long he sat in Turnbull's office. Time seemed of no relevance or importance to him now. When he finally managed to gain control of his emotions, he opened the letter he'd been given.

NESWELL GENERAL HOSPITAL

Friday

Hello Mark,

Thought I had better drop you a line to let you know that the Doctor's here are going to operate on me leg this morning. What a shock, eh man! Can you imagine how I felt when they told me I would lose part of me leg? It just ain't fair, is it? Although I suppose it will give Imran a chance now to open the bowling for you on Saturday, won't it? Anyway, Mark, it's got to be done to prevent the disease from spreading further. So don't you go worrying about me now, and remember what I said earlier about concentrating on the cricket match on Saturday and make sure you win, that's all. Cos if you don't, man, I'm just going to have to give you a kick up the backside with me stump, see if I don't. You got that? I got to go now, captain. I shall be thinking of you. Don't worry now, cos I'm going to be just fine once they sort me out. So long, pal.

> *From your best friend Wes.*

PS I ain't allowed any visitors apart from me folks for a couple of days.

With tears streaming down his face, Mark got to his feet and made his way out of Turnbull's office. What an awful thing to happen to your best mate, he thought to himself despairingly as he walked blindly out of the school. And not being allowed to see him made the situation even worse. What *must* poor Wes be going through? God! What a tragedy.

Mark suddenly found himself sitting in a pew at the back of his church after entering the building through a side door entrance. It was in this Catholic Church that both he and Wesley would make their confirmation together later that year. Mark felt drawn here now, sensing he would be nearer to his friend in these surrounds than anywhere else at this time of crisis for him.

He knelt down and gazed above him at the large wooden crucifix of the Lord positioned high above the altar.

"*Why,* Lord?" he questioned the daunting effigy out loud.

Then, sobbing profusely, repeated more angrily and more loudly: "*Why* . . . ? *Oh, why* . . . ?" as he buried his head in his hands in sheer frustration at not being given an explanation or reason for his friend's dilemma, his voice echoing through the church.

He remained kneeling for quite some considerable time before regaining any form of composure. Then, sitting upright, uttered defiantly, "How *could* you let this awful thing happen to my friend Wesley, God? I'll *never* forgive you for allowing this."

Mark began reading his pal's letter to him again. "And how on *earth* am I supposed to carry on with this cricket match tomorrow without him, pray? It wouldn't be right, would it? *None* of it."

But at that moment he realized he would have to do just the opposite, wouldn't he? The game *had* to go ahead as arranged, hadn't it? There were too many people involved for it not to now. And besides, his pal would never forgive him if he gave up at this stage of proceedings, would he?

"All right, Wes, you win!" he uttered out loud, rising to his feet as more tears filled his reddened eyes. "But I wanna come and see you at the hospital just as soon as I'm allowed after the game, do you hear?"

He made his way slowly out of the church, glancing over his shoulder up at the crucifix once more as he did so. "Take care of Wesley for me, Lord, won't you, please?" he whispered, making the sign of the cross before departing.

CHAPTER FOURTEEN

Opening Ceremony and Cricket Match

Mark rose early the following morning, the day of the long awaited Neswell School cricket match having finally arrived. He knew there would be a great deal to attend to prior to its start. He had gone to bed early the night previous because he was so upset at Wesley's predicament, as indeed were his parents and his Uncle Frank also. They obviously knew how much he was hurting and therefore had refrained from indulging in any unnecessary conversation with him.

Of course, everyone who knew young Wesley was absolutely shattered to hear of the terrible news. However, both Mark's father and his uncle emphasised the need for him to continue with what he and Wesley had started. Mark had even received a phone call from Mr Jackson at the hospital upon his arrival home yesterday afternoon imploring him on behalf of his son to make certain the game went ahead as planned at the school, and for him to obtain autographs from all the celebrities present. This request, he assured Wesley's father, he would do without fail for his pal.

"Oh, one more thing Wesley says you can do."

"What's that, Mr Jackson?" Mark was only too willing to offer his assistance at such a tragic time.

There was a long pause before the man finally declared with heartfelt emotion: "He told me ... He said to tell you that ... That you *must* try and win this first game for the school ..."

"Sure – sure thing, Mr Jackson," Mark promised the man tearfully.

And today as Mark made his way along the tree-lined entrance to their school, he was determined that the cricket team they had helped form together over the past few weeks would do just that for him.

The first person he met as he walked across the cricket field in the bright sunlight was Mick, the head groundsman from Lord's who was busy mowing the wicket for the game later.

"Hello, Mark!" the man greeted him with a warm smile, bringing his machine to a halt.

Mark was surprised he remembered his name at all after only meeting him briefly just that once with Wesley at Lord's that time.

"Hello!" Mark returned his smile, grateful for his expert help in preparing the school pitch on such a momentous occasion.

"It's a nice day for the match."

"It certainly is."

"I-I am so sorry to hear about your friend."

Mark wondered how this sun-tanned man from London had come to learn of poor Wesley's tragedy.

"The Headmaster told me when I arrived this morning," Mick explained. "That's tough – really tough. If there's anything I can do . . .?"

"Thanks." Mark felt the tears welling up in his eyes. "I-I'll leave you to it then."

"Sure thing, skipper. You have the cricket stumps for the match I take it?"

"Yes, my father's bringing them along."

"Right, have a good game then, young fella."

"We will, and thanks for helping."

The man looked him in the eye, placing a hand on his shoulder. "I wouldn't have missed it for the world, lad. I admire what you and your brave friend have achieved and wish you every success with it. Keep up the good work."

Mark knew this was fine praise indeed from one involved in the game at such a high level.

"And, Mark – when you next see Wesley – give him my kindest regards and tell him that both of you are welcome to come to Lord's anytime to watch Middlesex play. Just ask for me at the gate, okay?"

"Okay."

The groundsman then set his mower into motion again to continue the work at hand, while Mark left him to get on with it. He much appreciated what he had said, especially the part about going to Lord's. Wesley sure would be pleased to hear that. It was certainly something for him to look forward to once he got over his terrible ordeal. Mark knew now though that he must put out of his mind any thoughts of what his best pal must be going through and to just concentrate with the playing of this cricket match which lay ahead of him and his school.

Soon, his father, mother and his uncle would be arriving, he, having gone on ahead to be away from everything and on his own for a while to get some fresh air on this beautiful, bright sunny morning. He could hardly believe the day had finally arrived when his school would play cricket again after such a long absence. In little more than an hour his dream of this would be a reality. All the hard work in bringing this to fruition would have been well worth the effort by everyone.

However, he was finding it very hard to accept what had happened to Wes and of how much he would liked to have played alongside him today. It left him feeling very bitter and he hoped in his heart of hearts that it would not spoil the day for him.

"Good morning, Adams!" the cheerful voice of his headmaster greeted him as he emerged from a side door of the Staff Room. "This is the day you've been waiting for, eh?"

"It is, yes, sir!" Mark agreed happily, regaining his composure once more.

"You'll find the Staff Room all ready to accommodate your teams. I've brought in some more chairs for them to use."

"Thank you very much, sir."

79

It was then that Turnbull placed a friendly arm round Mark's shoulder. "I do know how you must be feeling about your friend, Mark, and I know that I speak on behalf of the school when I say that we are all so sorry to learn of what's happened to young Wesley. And if there is anything we can do to help, don't hesitate to ask, will you?"

Mark appreciated the headmaster's kind words. "No, I won't. Thank you, sir."

"Under the present circumstances you will understand that Mr Jackson won't be umpiring today, Mark, so I've agreed to instead. If *that's* all right with you, of course?"

Mark never thought he would ever see the day when the head of his school would volunteer to officiate a cricket match in this way, considering how much the man had opposed any such notion of even having a school side to begin with. And now, here he was actually asking Mark's permission to do so. It was all so unbelievable really.

"Yes, you do have my permission, sir!" Mark jokingly replied with a cheeky smile on his face.

"Right, well, I look forward to partnering your uncle later. Ten-thirty start, isn't it?"

"Yes, ten-thirty, sir."

Mark's relatives were the next to arrive on the scene. His mother had to organise and arrange the drinks and food she had carefully prepared to be consumed in the gymnasium between innings. His father would assist her and make sure all the Kwik-Cricket sets his company had donated were on display for other schools interested in putting them to good use. His Uncle Frank was going to insure that everything to do with the match would run smoothly before the teams actually took to the field. He would welcome the Middlesex skipper and the rest of his team personally. Also, the newspaper reporters and television personnel who had done so much between them to publicise this event, he would show the utmost hospitality. The BBC radio cricket commentator, Trevor Sinclair, confirmed his availability for the day, which, Frank thought, was certainly another attraction for all cricket lovers coming along to actually have the chance see this renowned celebrity in the flesh.

Within the next fifteen minutes the cricket teams arrived to participate in this momentous game along with parents, relatives, friends and neighbours from both the Neswell and Northwick schools, which also included a large populous from the surrounding Asian and West Indian communities. Uncle Frank's comment that this cricket match was doing more to promote race relations in the area than any of the other recognised bodies was most probably true.

With only a short while to go before the start of the game, the Middlesex County Cricket Club coach arrived at the school with a large contingent of players on board. True to his promise to Mr Jackson, Mark made sure he secured the signatures of all these players after being introduced to them by his uncle. Then the County captain, Nick Gallon, on behalf of his team conveyed deepest concern to Mark for his pal, Wesley, and promised they would all come and see him just as soon as he was well enough to receive visitors.

The cricket commentator and former England Test player, Trevor Sinclair, was next in line to be introduced to Mark, and then the two headmasters of both schools involved in this venture. Mr Sinclair congratulated Mark on his success in bringing today's game about, and informed him that he himself had always been a strong advocator of the softball approach to cricket at this particular level. "I *do* hope it catches on in other schools up and down the country, young man," he added encouragingly.

A surprise visitor to then appear on the scene was the Mayor of Wufton as he stepped down from his chauffeur-driven car with his chain of office glinting in the morning sunlight.

"I never knew *he* was supposed to be here today," Frank spoke out the corner of his mouth to his young nephew standing beside him before going across to welcome this official.

"I'll say this much for you, Adams," Turnbull, positioned the other side of Mark, uttered in admiration for his pupil. "Your game of cricket has managed to bring our Mayor to this school at long last. I've been trying for years to get him to attend functions here without any success whatsoever. Congratulations, my boy!''

''Me, too,'' Mark heard the head of Northwick Junior mumble rather despondently from further down the line of personnel who had gathered on the edge of the playing field to be introduced to the various celebrities.

''And now here he is turning up without even an invite,'' Turnbull added with wry amusement.

The *Out And About* television programme for whom young Mark and Wesley had given an interview were present and making themselves busy televising proceedings. There were newspaper reporters – both local and national – busy capturing the event for their many readers.

It was at this point that Mark became very emotional and had to fight hard to hold back tears as the thought of his best pal entered his mind. Poor Wes was missing all this, wasn't he? he pondered sadly. It was such a pity, because he deserved to be present to witness this memorable event for their school. It brought home to Mark how very cruel life can indeed be, and of how hard he was finding it to accept the tragedy that had cut short his friend's sporting potential in this way.

The mayor began addressing the large crowd gathered to watch these preliminary proceedings, speaking through a microphone that someone had placed at his disposal for the occasion.

At this point Mark's parents joined his company to stand one either side of him.

''Are you feeling all right, dear – you look a little pale?'' his mother asked quietly.

''We're a little concerned for you,'' his father added discretely.

Mark took a deep breath to regain his composure. ''I-I'm fine,'' he assured them. ''Just a little worried about Wesley, that's all.''

''The poor boy is in all our thoughts right now, dear.''

''*Shoosh*!'' an agitated voice belonging to a Town Hall official reprimanded his parents for daring to talk during the mayor's speech.

"Yes, I do think that both these youngsters are to be congratulated for bringing the game of cricket back here to Neswell School once again. . ."

"*Hear! Hear!*" an elderly gent from the crowd in front agreed with the mayor's statement.

". . .Speaking as a formal pupil at Neswell myself, I couldn't be more delighted at the decision by the school authorities to allow this *most* English of games to be played here once again. . ."

"Former pupil, indeed!" Turnbull murmured from the corner of his mouth to the headmaster of Northwick School.

"So that's the reason for his sudden interest in your School, Turnbull," came a curt reply from this man.

"*Shoosh!*"

This last exclamation from the Town Hall official brought forth sniggers of amusement from the majority of pupils in attendance, because an utterance of this nature would normally be targeted at them for misbehaving and not at the respective head teachers of the two schools about to participate in this cricket match. Mark's parents also joined in with the youngster's hilarity, both chuckling quietly to themselves.

However, this prevailing jocularity was soon to disappear as the Mayor continued with his speech in a more sombre manner.

"To those of you who may not already know, I have indeed some very sad news to relate regarding the plight of young Wesley Jackson, a pupil here at Neswell. For as I speak, he is lying in our local hospital recovering from a very serious operation that unfortunately has cost him his right leg."

Gasps of disbelief came from those without knowledge of this awful tragedy, and some of the pupils openly cried upon hearing the news. Parents looked at each other in shocked silence.

Young Mark stood with his head bowed low as a sign of respect for his pal.

"I know I speak on behalf of everyone," the mayor continued

seriously, "when I say that with the advent of today's cricket match taking place here between these two teams, I would like, on behalf of all present, to offer a sincere thank you to both the Neswell pupils responsible for making this all possible. Ladies and gentlemen! A big round of applause, please, for Mark Adams and Wesley Jackson."

This announcement was met with spontaneous applause from the gathered crowd for the two schoolboys in question.

"We're so proud of you, Mark, dear," Mrs Adams said to her son with excitement above the noise and commotion.

"Yes, very proud," Mark's father added as he joined in with the applause. "You and Wesley have achieved what you both set out to do. Well done, Son!"

Uncle Frank came through the crowd to congratulate his nephew on his success. "Just remember though that this is only the beginning, Mark," he cautioned the lad as he shook him warmly by the hand. "What you and your friend have done is just great. But now comes the hard work with future fixtures to arrange to ensure the game will catch on at other schools up and down the country."

"My brother is right, Son," Mark's father agreed. "No looking back now for you. So if there is anything at all your uncle or I can do to help further your cause, you have only to ask, okay?"

At that precise moment young Mark felt he was probably the happiest person alive in the whole world. At the same time though he was also probably the saddest because of his friend's tragic circumstances. He would dearly have loved Wesley to be present to celebrate this momentous occasion with him. But this was now a sheer impossibility and realized his main concern now was to concentrate on the job at hand to make a success of it. Wesley would certainly want him to, especially after all their hard work together in getting this far with it.

"I think you and Frank have helped enough," he said to his father, appreciative of all their efforts. "And thanks for donating all the Kwik-Cricket kits, Dad."

"May I say on behalf of my company and myself that it has

84

been a pleasure to help out in this way, Son,'' his father replied, smiling. ''And while on the subject, I would like to say how grateful I am to you for having opened my eyes to a lot of things lately, Mark. You have certainly taught me not to always put work before pleasure, that's for sure.''

Mark felt a lump come to his throat at these words from his father. He turned to face his uncle. ''And I can't thank you enough either, Uncle Frank,'' he said to him, his voice full of emotion.

Frank looked long and hard at him for a moment, before answering: ''It was the least I could do for someone who has the love of the game at heart like you. . .''

''*And* Wesley . . .?'' interrupted Mark, not wanting his friend's help in the matter to be overlooked.

''Yes, of course – *and* Wesley – we mustn't leave him out, must we?''

''Aren't you forgetting someone else, Mark?'' his father teased him.

Mark gazed about him. ''Oh, and for Nick Gallon and the Middlesex team for coming here to support us and our cause,'' he added excitedly.

''No, no. . . This person has given a great deal of their time and effort in helping towards your success, Son . . . ?''

Suddenly, the penny dropped. Of course, who else? ''*MUM!*'' he exclaimed loudly, not particularly minding who might hear him admit this, and hurrying over to give her a big thank you hug for all she had done to help.

''Maybe you should reserve judgement until after you're teas,'' Mrs Adams chuckled light heartedly, returning her son's loving embrace.

''I'm sure they've no need to worry on that score if what you've prepared is anything like you did for our day out at Lord's, Mary,'' her brother in law praised her efforts. ''Which reminds me – I never did thank you for . . .''

''All that remains for me to do now,'' the Mayor of Wufton's voice echoed out over the loudspeaker, cutting short Frank's worthy tribute to the lady in question, "is to thank everyone for having given their time to support this return of cricket to Neswell Junior School. I believe special thanks are due to Nick Gallon and the Middlesex team for honouring us with their presence here today. And also to the Lord's groundsman for travelling down to prepare the actual wicket for the game. And last, but not least, to the BBC radio cricket commentator and ex England bowler, Trevor Sinclair, for showing an interest in this project . . ."

"*Hear! Hear!*" our mutual friend agreed again jubilantly.

". . .I would also especially like to thank both Headmasters of the two schools involved very much for their support in all of this, without whose help today's cricket match would not have been possible. . ."

"Three cheers for Mr Turnbull and Mr Grimbald! Hip! Hip . . . !"

"*Hooray . . . !*"

"Hip! Hip . . . !"

"*Hooray . . . !*"

"Hip! Hip . . . !"

"*Hooray . . . !*"

". . . May I now call upon our two respective cricket captains to take to the field to make the toss for the start of this historical match."

Amid exuberant applause from the crowd, the two young school captains then strode proudly out to the wicket to undertake this task.

"Well, this is what you've been waiting for," Mark told himself excitedly. "This is what you and Wes set out to do. The dream we both had of playing cricket at our School has finally arrived."

"*Heads!*" Rusmat Khan, the young Pakistan skipper of Northwick School called as Mark, the home side captain, spun a silver coin into the air after they had shaken hands.

The coin fell face upwards on the green turf. "Heads it is," said Mark, bending down to retrieve it.

"We'll bat."

Five minutes later the first game of cricket to be played in over six years was allowed to take place once again on the sports field of Neswell Junior School.

Standing proudly in his fielding position at mid off in brilliant sunshine the captain of this school, young Mark Adams, sighed with happiness as he heard his headmaster, Mr Turnbull, give the go ahead for the match to commence, by proclaiming in a clear, authoritative umpiring voice: "PLAY!"

CHAPTER FIFTEEN

Capturing Posterity

Mark's teacher was rather pleased with the fact that he had not been called upon to umpire the cricket match at his school that day by the headmaster after all. The reason he had managed to escape this duty was because of an arrangement he had made with Mr Turnbull to record the whole of the proceedings on his home video camera in return for which he would be excused this most hazardous of tasks.

"Good thinking, Mr Fox," the head said, after hearing his suggestion. "This will mean capturing the match on film for posterity. Wonderful! Yes, I think your talents are best suited in this way rather than as an umpire, don't you?"

"I think so, Mr Turnbull." Mr Fox was convinced they were. He would much prefer this option to the alternative, that's for sure. "I can also make a copy for young Wesley to see when he is well enough?"

"Excellent! In fact, Mr Fox, you can do several copies if you like. The school can then sell the videos to those interested in purchasing them. Great way of raising funds for Neswell, don't you think?"

So, earlier that morning, Mr Fox arrived at Neswell along with his recording equipment to set this up in readiness for the big event. He occupied the small gardener's shed adjacent to the cricket field for this purpose, where an excellent view of the game could be had.

He captured all of the preliminary proceedings leading up to the actual game as they unfolded. The arrival of the Lord's groundsman to prepare the wicket: of young Mark's appearance on the scene: of Mr Turnbull, his wife, and the rest of the school team, accompanied by parents and friends to support Neswell: of the Middlesex players as they filed out of a coach. And, of course, the mayor and his entourage, followed by his speech after numerous introductions. The emotional response to Wesley's condition was also caught on film, as was a close up of the two school captains as they tossed a coin for the start of the game.

Then, it was down to the serious business of filming the cricket itself, with Northwick Junior electing to bat first after winning the toss in the twenty overs a side match. They got off to a reasonable start, and, after the first five overs, had scored twenty runs without loss. The opening Neswell fast bowling attack, although fairly accurate at times, failed to bother the opposing batsmen very much. In fact, Wesley's replacement delivered two no balls and a wide in his opening spell, which didn't much please his skipper, Mark Adams. So he brought his spinners into the attack, after which two quick wickets were to fall. However, despite this breakthrough, the middle order batsmen began putting on a stand together and took advantage of some loose spin bowling by hitting a succession of boundaries between them.

At intervals, Mr Fox would focus his video camera onto the small, wooden scoreboard positioned opposite in the corner of the field to keep check on the score and fall of wickets, this piece of apparatus having only been located earlier in the gardener's shed along with its box of cobweb-covered metal numbers after some frantic searching by everyone. The score at that particular moment showed the visitors as having made eighty-five for the loss of two wickets off twelve overs.

Even Mr Fox, with his somewhat limited knowledge of the game of cricket, knew that Neswell desperately needed another wicket and to also stem the run rate to ensure that they would not be chasing too bigger a total themselves.

He moved back to the field of play and concentrated on Mark,

89

his pupil and skipper of Neswell as the lad tried various bowling changes and manoeuvring of his fielders in the hope of breaking up the partnership of the Northwick middle order pair. This was where the skills of captaincy were needed, and it certainly would be an exercise in learning the many aspects of this exacting craft for him. But, having tried all the resources at his command, it proved to be of no avail as the two youngsters continued to domineer the crease, until finally amassing an impressive total of one hundred and forty five with no further loss of wicket from their allocated twenty overs. Sixty of these runs came from the last twelve overs; with the number four bat finishing on fifty-four not out, this magnificent effort being given enthusiastic applause by everyone.

During the course of the Northwick innings, Mr Fox also devoted some time at the end of an over to zoom in on certain sections of the crowd to capture their reactions and comments, especially those of the Middlesex celebrities seated just down from him on the right. "Oh, good shot!" "Well fielded, Mark!" "Well bowled, young 'un!" "Good innings! Well played!"

But for now, it was time for the tea interval – even though it was still only mid morning – with everyone heading off in the direction of the gymnasium to sample Mary's tuna and cucumber sandwiches, homemade fruitcake, lemonade and cups of tea.

Even here, Mr Fox made time for further video recording.

"I see ol' Foxy is doing a video of the match then?" one of Mark's team commented, munching his sandwich and guzzling pop.

"Yeah, I believe he offered to, instead of umpiring," Mark explained. "My uncle stood in his place."

"Be great though, won't it – seeing ourselves on film?" another of the team said excitedly.

"Lovely tea, Mrs Adams," Mr Turnbull, sitting alongside the mayor, complimented her.

"Excellent!" someone else agreed.

"Neswell will have their work cut out getting these runs," Mr Adams stated in conversation with his brother. "They certainly missed young Wesley's bowling all right."

"Yes, I must have a quick word with Mark before his team goes out to bat," replied Frank, sipping tea.

The two Neswell Junior opening batsmen strode out to the wicket after the tea interval amid spectator applause, while Mr Fox continued to film proceedings once again from his position in the gardener's shed. Mark's uncle managed to speak a few words with his nephew during the break to explain the absolute need for his side to attack the Northwick Junior bowlers right from the onset if they were to stand any chance at all of scoring the run rate being asked of them to secure victory.

However, Neswell got off to a disastrous start, losing three quick wickets during the first four overs. With only fourteen runs on the board, Mark came to the wicket to join his Asian number three bat, Imran, a very good, fast scoring player who had made ten by then. Together, they began to score more rapidly as they proceeded to attack the bowling with an array of shots all round the wicket, which included many boundaries amongst them. People watching were becoming excited as the prospect that Neswell might possibly be on course to perhaps winning the match dawned on them as these two batsmen brought the hundred partnership up between them.

"Well played, Neswell!" The Middlesex captain was on his feet cheering with the rest of his team. "Keep going! Keep going!"

At this stage, Mr Fox became very excited also. "You can win, Neswell!" he shouted between filming. "Come on, Mark! Do it for Wesley! Do it for your friend!"

But with six overs remaining and needing thirty runs to win, Imran was caught out on the boundary after having scored a brilliant sixty-five. The next incoming batsman was immediately in trouble from his very first delivery, having called to his captain for a short run, but then not quite making his ground in time as a sharp throw from the extra cover fielder made direct contact with the stumps, leaving the umpire, Mr Turnbull, with no other option but to give this batsman out. Neswell's score stood at one hundred and fifteen for the loss of six wickets.

Foxy's heart began to beat faster as he filmed the next school batsman to arrive at the crease. Another wicket to fall now would be disastrous for Neswell, he thought to himself fearfully. But his fears of this happening were soon laid to rest as this young fellow cracked his first two deliveries to the boundary for four runs. Great stuff indeed, that had everyone jumping around with excitement.

In fact, the captain, together with his new partner, saw the last remaining overs through without too much difficulty, and, between them, and with two balls to spare, scored the required runs needed for their school to win the match in a nail-biting finish, with Mark just managing to complete his half century.

On doing so, he said quietly to himself and with deep felt emotion: *"That's for you, Wes! Just for you!"*

His fine achievement was greeted with tumultuous applause by everyone, as was the tremendous victory over Northwick Junior as the players trooped off the field. Congratulations on his and his team's performance were offered personally to him by all the Middlesex players, and from Trevor Sinclair and the mayor before they departed. And, of course, from his parents and uncle. And then from Mr Turnbull and the staff of Neswell. The one person he felt who should be receiving as much of the accolade as he for his work in all of this was without doubt his pal Wesley Jackson. He was sure though that Mr Turnbull would make mention of this at assembly on Monday morning, along with a detailed description of their exciting win over Northwick.

Yes, a truly remarkable finish to a memorable game of cricket that had been brought about by the sheer determination of two young schoolboys because of their love for the game which had now been captured on video for all to see by Mr Fox, the person who had strongly objected to it taking place at all in the first place, but who would now confess to having become thoroughly engrossed in the match and for also having participated in it the way he had.

Mark couldn't wait for a copy of his teacher's video to take to the hospital to show Wesley.